The intercom clicked, and once more their principal's voice came through. "The seniors have also chosen their court. Our kings and queens will be attended by juniors Jayden O'Connor" — Shelby let out a shrill squeal — "and Adrianna Tolle; sophomores Michael Evans and Kathleen Lambright; and ..."

Katy didn't hear the rest of the principal's announcement. Her ears began to ring, and the room seemed to spin. The seniors had chosen her as the sophomore representative for the homecoming court. Jewel had said only popular kids were chosen — and they had chosen *her*. She broke out in a cold sweat, hardly aware of the open-mouthed gawks of her classmates.

How could she possibly miss homecoming now?

Katy's Homecoming

Kim Vogel Sawyer

KATY LAMBRIGHT SERIES

ZONDERVAN®

ZONDERVAN.com/
AUTHORTRACKER
follow your favorite authors

ZONDERVAN

Katy's Homecoming
Copyright © 2011 by Kim Vogel Sawyer

This title is also available as a Zondervan ebook.
Visit www.zondervan.com/ebooks

Requests for information should be addressed to:
Zondervan, *Grand Rapids, Michigan* 49530

Library of Congress Cataloging-in-Publication Data

Sawyer, Kim Vogel.
    Katy's homecoming / Kim Vogel Sawyer.
        p. cm. — (Katy Lambright series)
        ISBN 978-0-310-72287-8 (softcover)
        1. Mennonites—Juvenile fiction. [1. Mennonites—Fiction. 2. Christian life—Fiction.
3. Individuality—Fiction. 4. Dating (Social customs)—Fiction. 5. High schools—Fiction.
6. Schools—Fiction. 7. Family life—Kansas—Fiction. 8. Kansas—Fiction.] I. Title.
PZ7.S26832Kaj 2011
    [Fic]—dc22   2010032815

All Scripture quotations, unless otherwise indicated, are taken from the Holy Bible, *King James Version.*

Any Internet addresses (websites, blogs, etc.) and telephone numbers printed in this book are offered as a resource. They are not intended in any way to be or imply an endorsement by Zondervan, nor does Zondervan vouch for the content of these sites and numbers for the life of this book.

Published in association with Hartline Literary Agency, Pittsburgh, Pennsylvania 15235.

Cover design: Kris Nelson
Cover photography: Marc Raines
Interior design: Carlos Eluterio Estrada, Greg Johnson/Textbook Perfect

Printed in the United States of America

10 11 12 13 14 15 /DCI/ 23 22 21 20 19 18 17 16 15 14 13 12 11 10 9 8 7 6 5 4 3 2 1

For Kristian, Kaitlyn, and Kamryn—
No matter what hardships intrude upon your life's
journeys,
may you always discover a reason to dance.

To every thing there is a season,
and a time to every purpose under the heaven:
... a time to mourn, and a time to dance.
Ecclesiastes 3:1, 4b

Chapter One

Why did some girls act so goofy when boys were around? And who would've guessed Shelby Nuss would become one of the goofy ones?

Katy Lambright coiled one of the ribbons trailing from her mesh hair covering around her finger and tried not to stare as her best friend from Salina High North leaned over to bump shoulders with her boyfriend. Shelby's streaky blonde hair fell across her cheek, and she tucked it behind her ear while releasing a giggle — the kind of giggle she'd never used before she started dating Jayden O'Connor. The flirty sound carried from the other end of the table and rang over all the other cafeteria noise.

Katy was used to her best friend from home, Annika, giggling whenever Caleb Penner came around, but Shelby had always been more ... mature. Katy wasn't sure she liked this new, giggly, giddy Shelby who grabbed every available second with Jayden instead of hanging out with Katy, Cora, and Trisha like she used to.

A loud huff interrupted Katy's thoughts. She shifted to look at Cora, who sat directly across the table with Trisha.

Cora made a sour face and nudged Trisha with her elbow. "It's getting nauseating. I might start sitting at a different table for lunch if they're going to be, like, all over each other while I'm trying to eat."

Trisha snorted, pushing shriveled peas around on her plate with her fork. "You were just as overboard in the PDA department when you went out with Brett last year."

"Was not!"

"Were too," Trisha insisted. She turned to Katy. "You think Shelby and Jayden are bad? Cora almost sat in Brett's lap she snuggled so close. You couldn't have slipped a blade of grass between them. Honestly, it was totally gross."

Cora smacked Trisha's arm. "Trisha, you're so mean!" But then she laughed.

Katy focused on her lunch while Cora and Trisha chatted with each other. The two girls had always been close, but they'd become even tighter in the past month since their friend Bridget moved away after Christmas. Even though Katy sometimes envied their BFF status, she'd still had Shelby to talk to, so it hadn't mattered that much.

Another giggle rang, piercing Katy's ears. She frowned. *Until Jayden came along and changed everything . . .* Wasn't it enough to face all of the changes happening at home with Dad getting ready to marry Mrs. Graber and Annika trying to convince Caleb Penner to court her? Katy needed things at school to stay the same.

She finished her last swallow of milk and curled her hands around her tray, eager to leave the cafeteria, when someone yanked out the chair next to her. Shelby flung herself into the seat. To Katy's relief, Jayden was nowhere in sight.

Shelby crowed, "Guess what!"

Trisha and Cora shrugged in unison. Katy said, "What?"

Shelby hunched her shoulders and giggled. "Jayden just asked me to the homecoming dance—and I said yes!"

Both Trisha and Cora squealed. Katy almost rolled her eyes. Just minutes ago they had called Shelby's behavior nauseating. Now they were excited? She said, "What's the homecoming dance?"

Cora gawked at Katy. "Oh, come on, Katy. I mean, even if Mennonites don't actually do it, you have to know what a dance is."

Katy's ears heated. Of course she knew what it meant to dance. And Cora was right—no one in Katy's fellowship ever danced. Dad had caught her swirling around the kitchen when she was eight or nine, pretending to be a leaf caught in the wind, and he'd thought she was dancing. He had sat her down and had a firm talk about the difference between appropriate and inappropriate movements. "I know what dancing is. But what's homecoming?"

Shelby caught Katy's wrist. "Every year, during basketball season, all of the alumni—"

Katy made a puzzled face. "Alumni?"

Shelby went on as if Katy hadn't interrupted. "—are invited back to Salina High North for a game. We usually schedule it when we're playing one of our biggest rivals. So this year it's the very last game of the season, against Salina High West."

Trisha, Cora, and Shelby all broke into a chanted chorus. "Let's show West: We're the best! *Goooooo*, North!" They all laughed.

At that moment Jewel, the foster girl who lived with Shelby's family, wandered by. She stopped and sent a sarcastic look around the circle of girls. "What's with the cheerleader act?"

"We're telling Katy about homecoming," Trisha said. "Shelby's going to the dance with Jayden."

"Jayden O'Connor?" Jewel asked.

"Who else?" Shelby wriggled in her chair, flashing a huge smile.

Tossing her long dyed-orange hair over her shoulder, Jewel released a little snort. "Big deal. Jayden's just a junior. *I* plan on going with a senior — Tony Adkins."

Katy didn't know Tony Adkins, but she'd seen him in the halls and had heard all about him. He was the star of the school's football team, and half the girls in school thought he was handsome enough to be a movie star. But Katy had also heard he liked to party — and not the kinds of parties the young people in her town of Schellberg enjoyed. She couldn't imagine Shelby's parents allowing Jewel to go out with a boy like that.

Trisha's eyes popped. "Tony Adkins asked you to the homecoming dance?"

Jewel quirked her lips into a funny scowl. "Not yet. But he will."

"But —," Trisha started.

Katy shook her head, making her ribbons bounce. "Does *alumni* mean the students who've gone here before?"

Shelby nodded. "That's right. You wouldn't believe how crowded the bleachers get. It's always cool to see how many people come back."

Cora added, "But best of all, a senior boy and girl get crowned homecoming king and queen, and there's a whole court in attendance—the seniors choose a boy and girl from the junior, sophomore, and freshman classes to be part of the royalty." Suddenly, she jerked. "Hey! Homecoming's just two weeks away. I bet the seniors have already voted for their attendants. When do you think they'll announce all the candidates?"

Trisha shrugged. "Gotta be soon. Maybe tomorrow?"

"Ooooh, I can't wait!" Cora cupped her cheeks with her hands and sighed. "I've always wanted to be one of the attendants—or better yet, the queen when I'm a senior."

Jewel rolled her eyes. "Dream on. Only the really popular kids get to be attendants, kings, and queens. You hardly qualify as *popular.*" She sauntered off, ignoring Cora's deflated face.

Katy could make little sense of Cora's comment. Often she felt confused by the way they did things in the public high school. In Schellberg, their community school only went through the ninth grade, so they didn't have seniors or homecoming. But based on the excitement in Cora's tone, homecoming was a major deal. "So there's a king and queen, and lots of people come back for a basketball game, and then you go to a dance?"

"Uh-huh," Trisha said.

A bell rang, signaling the end of the lunch period. Katy piled her silverware and rumpled napkin on her tray and stood. Trisha stayed close, talking as they walked to the scraping table. "They clear the gym right after the game, and we use the basketball court for a dance floor. The whole school's invited, freshmen through seniors. Lots of the kids don't go, but I wouldn't miss it. Even if we don't have a date, we girls all get our hair and nails done, and we wear really beautiful dresses. It's so fun to get all dressed up. The guys look amazing in suits with ties and everything. It's really an awesome night, Katy — it doesn't end until midnight. Do you think you'll be able to come?"

Katy stacked her tray on the table and shifted out of the way of other students crowding up to get rid of their trays. Beautiful dresses? Dancing? Regret filled Katy's stomach. "No. My dad wouldn't approve."

Trisha pursed her lips. She linked arms with Cora, and the four girls headed for the lockers to retrieve their books for the afternoon classes. "That's too bad, 'cause ..." She and Cora exchanged smirks. "We heard a rumor."

Shelby scuttled to Trisha's side, nearly pushing Katy out of the way. "Trisha, don't you dare! He wants to be the one to talk to her!"

Cora and Trisha laughed. Katy's scalp prickled. What was going on?

"But isn't it better if she knows in advance?" Trisha said. "Especially since she said she won't be able to go. She can be planning how to — you know — let him down gently."

Katy grabbed Trisha's arm, bringing the girl to a halt. Cora and Shelby stopped too. They created a block in the middle of the hallway, but other students just filed around them. "What are you talking about? Letting who down about what?"

Cora covered her mouth with her hand and giggled. "We gotta tell her. It's not right to keep quiet."

Shelby threw her hands in the air. "I am not going to be a part of this." She stomped off.

Trisha and Cora jostled Katy to the wall, out of the way of the flow of students, then leaned in close. Katy understood how a mouse would feel when cornered by two hungry cats. Trisha said, "Be prepared, Katy. We heard that Bryce wants to ask you to homecoming."

Chapter Two

Katy grabbed her books and backpack from her locker and headed to class. Her feet scuffed, and her mind reeled. Bryce Porter—the same Bryce who made butterflies twirl in her stomach—wanted to ask her to the homecoming activities? But why hadn't he said anything? She saw him every day in English, history, and forensics. He'd just been his usual friendly self, the same way he was with everybody.

Maybe Trisha and Cora had heard wrong. But, deep down, she hoped they hadn't. Even though she would have to say no—even though Dad would *never* let her to go a school dance—she still hoped Bryce would ask. Then she could write in her journal, *Bryce Porter wanted to go to a dance with me.* She would cherish those words forever.

Katy sank into her seat just as the late bell rang. Her heart pounded so hard, she could hardly hear the algebra teacher's instruction. Her thoughts raced ahead to the end of the day and forensics class when she would see Bryce again. She pictured his red-blond spiky hair and lopsided grin. Although he wasn't movie-star handsome, like Tony Adkins, she liked the way Bryce looked. And she liked his voice — warm and casual, never sarcastic or gruff the way a lot of the boys were at times. She imagined how his voice would sound as he asked her to homecoming. It would probably get lower, both in volume and tone, because he would be a little shy and embarrassed. She scrunched her eyes, straining to hear his voice inside her head.

Someone tapped her on the shoulder, and Katy let out a squeak of surprise. She turned around. Marlys Horton, Bryce's forensics duet acting partner, was glaring at her. Katy had discovered during her weeks of being in debate and forensics with Marlys that the girl glared a lot. Sometimes for no good reason.

Marlys waved a stack of papers. "Take these, and pass them on up. Mr. Case is waiting."

Humiliation heated Katy's ears. She grabbed the pages, added her own completed assignment to the stack, and passed them to the person in front of her. She needed to pay attention before she got in trouble with the teacher. But it was very hard to think about rationals and polynomials when she might be asked to a homecoming game and dance in less than three hours.

After algebra, Shelby and Katy walked out of class together. "They told you, didn't they?"

Katy knew who and what. She nodded.

Shelby sighed. "I thought so. I saw how distracted you were in algebra. Katy, listen ..." She caught Katy's arm and drew her to the edge of the hallway but kept walking so they wouldn't be late to their next class. "He might not say anything. He and I talked a couple days ago — "

Bryce and Shelby had talked about her? The uncomfortable thought put a funny taste in Katy's mouth. She swallowed hard.

" — and I told him I didn't think Mennonites were allowed to dance. So he might not ask. I know you like him." Shelby dropped her voice to a whisper and glanced around. Katy looked around too. She hoped no one was listening to their conversation. She would die if someone overheard them and then ran to tell Bryce she liked him! "But don't be disappointed if he doesn't ask you. 'Cause if he doesn't ask, it's only to keep you from getting into trouble with your dad, okay?"

Katy nodded, but she knew she would be disappointed if he didn't ask. People — especially people like Marlys and Jewel — looked at her and saw only her Mennonite dress and cap. They saw her as different. Even weird. But if Bryce asked her to the dance, it would mean he saw *Katy*, a girl like any other girl in the school. Of all the students in Salina High North, she wanted Bryce to see her the same as anybody else.

She followed Shelby into art appreciation, determined to pay better attention than she had in algebra. But she couldn't stay focused. She glanced at the clock again and again, amazed at how slowly it moved. When would she be able to go to forensics and see Bryce? Would he ask her in front of everyone, or would he take her aside, maybe into the hallway? Would everyone else guess what he was doing? How would he react when she told him she wasn't allowed to dance? Would he then think she was weird, like so many other students thought? An afternoon had never stretched as long as this one.

A few minutes before the closing bell rang, the inter-com system clicked. Everyone looked up at the square box mounted above the teacher's desk and waited for the an-nouncement. The principal's scratchy voice came through.

"Students, as you know, our homecoming game against Salina High West will be the last Friday of the month, right here at Salina High North." He paused, and the class erupted into cheers. Katy's heart skipped a beat — the last Friday of the month, February 26. The day after Dad and Mrs. Graber's wedding. After a few seconds, the principal's voice sounded again. "The faculty has approved our se-nior royalty. The following students will serve as king and queen candidates ..."

The room fell silent while the principal called the names of four senior girls and four boys. Katy only recog-nized one name: Tony Adkins. Sympathy teased her; Jewel would certainly be disappointed. Why would a senior king candidate ask a sophomore girl to the homecoming dance?

Another pause allowed the students to applaud for the candidates. Then the teacher held up his hands to bring order. The intercom clicked, and once more their princi-pal's voice came through. "The seniors have also chosen their court. Our kings and queens will be attended by juniors Jayden O'Connor" — Shelby let out a shrill squeal — "and Adrianna Tolle; sophomores Michael Evans and Kathleen Lambright; and ..."

Katy didn't hear the rest of the principal's announce-ment. Her ears began to ring, and the room seemed to spin. The seniors had chosen her as the sophomore repre-sentative for the homecoming court. Jewel had said only popular kids were chosen — and they had chosen *her*.

She broke out in a cold sweat, hardly aware of the open-mouthed gawks of her classmates.

How could she possibly miss homecoming now?

Katy had a hard time sitting still as the bus carried her toward the intersection where Dad would pick her up. Usually the noisy voices of the younger kids irritated her, but today she ignored them. Her thoughts were all turned inward.

Bryce hadn't shown up at forensics. She'd overheard Marlys complaining about his mom making a dentist appointment during forensics time — didn't the woman know they needed to practice for the upcoming meet? Although Katy had hoped to see him, a part of her was almost relieved. She wasn't sure she could handle finding out she was the sophomore attendant *and* get asked to homecoming by a boy she really liked without melting into a puddle on the floor. By tomorrow, she would be used to the idea of being the attendant, then she could deal with Bryce's invitation. Assuming he really did ask her.

And why had the seniors chosen her? Even Trisha and Cora — although they acted happy for her — expressed their amazement that Katy had been given such an incredible honor. Katy didn't really care why she'd been chosen. She was just thrilled to have the chance. Finally — even if it was for only one day — she would be noticed. Accepted. A part of the popular crowd. Goosebumps broke out across her arms, and she hugged herself in delight.

She looked out the window as the bus approached the intersection. Instead of Dad's blue pickup, Mrs. Graber's black, old four-door Buick waited. The sight didn't surprise

Katy. Since Mrs. Graber and Dad would soon be husband
and wife, Mrs. Graber had begun taking some responsibility for Katy, including picking her up at the bus stop if
Dad was really busy with the dairy herd. But today Katy
wished Dad were there. She wanted him to be the first to
know about her being chosen as homecoming attendant.
Even though she was starting to like Mrs. Graber and had
given Dad her blessing on getting remarried, Dad would
always be first as far as Katy was concerned.

The bus creaked to a stop, and Katy hopped out. She
dashed to the car and realized Gramma Ruthie was sitting in the front passenger seat. So she climbed in behind
Gramma and gave her an awkward hug over the seat's
high back. Then she acknowledged Mrs. Graber. "Hi.
Thanks for picking me up."

Mrs. Graber turned the car around and headed down
the dirt road that led to Katy's farm. "Hi, Kathleen. Did
you have a good day?"

Mrs. Graber always asked the same question when
she picked up Katy from the bus stop. Katy wondered if
she was still a little uncomfortable or just unimaginative.
Either way, Katy answered politely, "I did, thank you." But
she didn't explain how good the day had been. Resting her
arms on the front seat, she leaned close to Gramma Ruthie.
"Are we going to your house, Gramma?"

Gramma shook her head, the black ribbons from her
cap swaying next to her wrinkly cheeks. "No, Katy-girl,
I'm coming to your house. Rosemary and I are making
mints for the wedding. You have that big deep freeze in
the basement to keep them in, so it makes more sense to
make them at your place."

Katy nodded. Usually the bride's family prepared the
food for a wedding celebration, but since Mrs. Graber
moved to Schellberg from Meschke, Kansas, and didn't
have any family close by, Gramma Ruthie had promised to
help. Katy had offered to help too, but most of the time, the
women shooed her out of the kitchen. In a way, she didn't
mind — she usually had homework to do. But in a way, it
bothered her. It felt strange to have another woman working in the kitchen that had been Katy's ever since she was
old enough to cook for Dad.

"Are you making the same kind of mints Ron and Taryn
Knepp had at their wedding?" Katy had enjoyed attend-
ing the wedding for Annika's older sister in mid-January.
She hoped she would end up having fun at Dad and Mrs.
Graber's wedding.

"The very same recipe," Gramma confirmed.

"Awesome! Those were epic."

Gramma Ruthie tipped her head and gave Katy a look
that was a cross between amusement and disapproval.
"Really, Katy-girl, the things you say."

Katy slid back in the seat. She tried not to bring school
words home to Schellberg, but sometimes they flew out
of her mouth before she could stop them. As Annika
and Katy's cousins Lola and Lori often pointed out, Katy
needed to be careful, or the deacons would worry she
was picking up too many worldly habits. Then she'd have
to stop attending the high school in Salina. "I just meant
the mints were very good. They were creamier than ones
we've had at other weddings."

Gramma smiled. "We liked them too. That's why we're
making them for Samuel and Rosemary."

"I hope we bought enough candy forms," Mrs. Graber said. "They're reusable, of course, but I don't know how long it takes for the candy to set up so they can be removed from the forms." The two women began discussing mint making, leaving Katy out of the conversation.

Katy leaned into the corner of the seat and let her mind wander to the moment when the principal announced her name as the sophomore attendant for homecoming. The other students in the room had looked at her in surprise, probably mirroring the stunned expression on her own face. No one congratulated her the way they had the boy attendant, Michael, but she didn't care. Just being chosen was so much more than she had ever expected. *Now if only Bryce would—*

She frowned, forcing herself to face the truth. Even though Dad would be happy for her, he would never let her buy a dress and put on makeup and leave her hair uncovered in public. And how could she possibly stand with all the other royalty in her Mennonite caped dress and mesh cap with its ribbons hanging alongside her cheeks? She would look ridiculous, and people would laugh. No, she wouldn't be able to actually be the attendant, so she should stop thinking about it.

Sadness struck so hard her eyes burned. She blinked several times to keep tears from forming. Maybe she wouldn't tell Dad at all, just to keep from hearing him say, "No, that's not something you can do, Katy-girl."

Mrs. Graber pulled her car beside the barn and turned off the engine. Katy reached for the door handle to let herself out, so she could escape to her bedroom and write all her frustration in her journal. But Mrs. Graber's voice stopped her.

"Oh! Kathleen, I nearly forgot. Your dad asked me to tell you we've decided to take a little trip — just a weekend one — after our wedding. Caleb Penner has agreed to take care of the cows for us, so you won't be needed here at the farm. Your dad thought you might like a little vacation of sorts too." She laughed lightly, her eyes crinkling at the corners. "So he plans to ask Shelby's father if you could spend the weekend with them. That is, if you want to stay in Salina with the Nusses. Would that be all right with you?"

Katy's sadness zipped away so quickly it almost made her dizzy. The wedding was the day before homecoming. If she stayed with Shelby, Katy could go to the same places Shelby went. And Katy knew where Shelby would be going. She answered quickly. "Sure. That would be fine with me if it's okay with Shelby's parents."

"Good. Your dad will go into the grocer and give them a call later this week then."

Katy bounced out of the car and headed for the house with Mrs. Graber and Gramma Ruthie trailing behind her. Guilt tried to pinch her conscience, but she pushed the feeling away. She wasn't going to get into any trouble. She'd be with Shelby. And Bryce. And for one night, she would get to find out how it felt to be a normal, popular girl.

Chapter Three

Katy hesitated before entering the forensics room the last hour on Thursday. She smoothed her hands over the skirt of her best dress, the purple dress Mrs. Graber had sewn for her Christmas present. She'd chosen it that morning because purple was a happy color but mostly because Annika had told Katy the purple made her eyes seem violet instead of blue. When Bryce asked her to homecoming, he'd probably lean close, and she wanted him to notice her violet eyes.

"Kathleen, out of the way." The bossy voice came from behind Katy. Katy skittered through the door so Marlys and a couple other forensics girls could go in too. Marlys flounced past Katy with her nose in the air. The other girls did the same.

Several of the sophomore girls had been snotty to Katy over the course of the day. Although she didn't like being ignored by the popular girls—usually they acted as if she didn't exist—being the target for snippy comments and condescending looks was even worse. Shelby had told her not to let it bother her—they were jealous because the seniors had chosen Katy as an attendant. "It's not you, Katy, really. It would be anybody who got picked. They'll get over it," Shelby had assured her. Katy hoped they'd get over it soon. Being constantly dissed was not fun.

Katy glanced around the room, but she didn't spot Bryce. She knew he was at school today because she'd seen him in earlier classes, the cafeteria, and the hallway. He'd smiled at her twice, but he hadn't tried to talk to her. Her hopes had risen and fallen so many times she felt like she'd been stuck on a roller coaster. Sighing, she slipped into a desk and opened her backpack. She removed her oration about relying on faith for strength to overcome hardship. She'd memorized the six-minute speech, but if she read it, she might be able to think about something besides Bryce. Bending over the page, she forced her eyes to focus on the first line: *Into every life, a little rain must fall—*

"Bryce!"

At Marlys's shrill cry, Katy turned her head so fast one of her ribbons smacked her on the jaw. Bryce strode into the room. His gaze found hers, and Katy held her breath. Would he come over to her desk to talk to her? But Marlys dashed across the floor and captured his arm.

"I thought you'd never show up. I got this great idea yesterday on staging, and I want to try it to see if it works better than what we planned before." Marlys dragged Bryce to the far corner of the classroom. He sent Katy an apologetic look but then turned his back and started working with Marlys. Katy watched for several minutes, hoping he might look at her again, but he didn't turn around.

Disappointed, Katy returned to her written speech. *Just*

*work, Katy. That's what you're here for—not for flirting
with Bryce.* She needed to be ready. On Thursdays the students performed for each other in preparation for weekend
meets. They never got through all of the performers because there were too many of them to fit into an hour, but
everyone needed to be prepared in case Mr. Gorsky drew
his or her name from the fishbowl on his desk.

Students milled around, chatting in small groups or
practicing. No one approached Katy's desk. She watched
out of the corner of her eye as Mr. Gorsky talked with
Bryce and Marlys. He gestured, pointing to various spots
on the floor, then Bryce and Marlys apparently tried what
he suggested. He nodded, and finally he turned to face the
entire class.

"All right, everyone, find a seat and let's quiet down.
Bryce and Marlys are going to do their duet act first — "

Marlys groaned, bending her knees as if she was going
to faint, but then she bounced up, slung her arm around
Bryce's shoulders, and giggled. Katy experienced a brief
stab of jealousy. Marlys was so at ease with boys. So was
Jewel, and even Shelby, although Shelby wasn't as flirty as
Jewel or Marlys. Katy bit her lower lip, battling feelings of
inadequacy. How did a girl learn to be comfortable around
boys? Katy had always felt a bit on edge with boys her age.
Of course, before the deacons had given her permission to
attend Salina High North, she'd only been around one boy
her age: Caleb Penner. And he could make anyone edgy
with his constant teasing.

Katy tried not to scowl when Marlys grabbed Bryce's
arm again and dragged him to the front of the classroom.
As soon as everyone was seated, Marlys stepped forward.

She put her hands behind her back and announced the title and author of their play. Then she and Bryce launched into their duet act about college students who visit a camp-site called Gilded Pond, only to discover it's in the middle of a swamp.

The play was humorous, and both Bryce and Marlys performed well, pretending to fight off king-size mosqui-toes and slog through mushy ground, but Katy didn't join the laughter with the other students. Seeing Bryce so close to Marlys created a lump of envy in her throat that she couldn't swallow. Years ago, she'd memorized a verse in Proverbs about envy being rottenness in a person's bones. She didn't want her bones to rot, but she also didn't want Marlys hanging on Bryce's elbow or leaping into his arms in an attempt to escape a make-believe crocodile. Not even if it was just part of a play.

When Bryce and Marlys finished, the students ap-plauded. Katy managed to offer a few half-hearted claps along with the others. The students called out their com-ments and suggestions for improving the performance, then Mr. Gorsky reached for the fishbowl. Seven other students performed, but Katy's name wasn't drawn. That suited her fine. Just being in the room with Bryce made her hands sweat and her heart pound. If she tried to stand in front of everyone and talk, she'd probably make a fool of herself.

At the end of class, Mr. Gorsky shared last-minute infor-mation about the upcoming Saturday meet in Minneapolis. He read through the list of students who'd signed up to attend, and Katy's heart gave another little leap when he read Bryce and Marlys's names together. Her name wasn't on the list—Dad had told her she needed to wait until

after the wedding to go to another forensics meet in case
Mrs. Graber needed help with the wedding preparations.
She wished she were going to Minneapolis, though. She'd
only competed twice so far this season, but she'd earned
a third-place medal in Marquette. She wanted to try for
a second- or even a first-place medal before the season
ended in late March.

The bell rang, and Mr. Gorsky said, "Brett and Taylor,
hold up—I need to talk to you for a minute. Everybody
else, see you tomorrow."

"'Bye, Mr. G!" students called as they jostled out the
door.

Katy returned her speech to her backpack then stood
to fling the bag over her shoulder. Her elbow bumped
somebody, and she turned to apologize. She discovered
Bryce standing next to her desk. Her stomach immediately
turned a somersault.

He rubbed his arm and grinned at her. "You've got a really pointy elbow."

"I'm so sorry!" She felt heat building in her ears.
Flustered to have him so close after wanting him to be
close all day, she stammered, "I—I didn't see you."

"How could you with me standing behind you? It's
okay."

If she'd jabbed Caleb Penner with her elbow, he'd do
everything he could to make her feel stupid about it. But
Bryce just told her it was okay. He was so nice. She tried
to think of something else to say. Jewel or Marlys would
know what to say. But Katy's tongue felt stuck to the roof
of her mouth. So she stood there as quietly as if she were
in church and waited for him to talk again.

He glanced over his shoulder at Mr. Gorsky and the two remaining students. Then he bobbed his head toward the door. "Can ... can I walk you to the bus?"

Katy noticed the tops of his ears had turned pink. Somehow the sight made her feel less embarrassed. She ducked her head so he wouldn't see her smile. "Sure. I need to go by my locker first, though."

"That's fine." They headed down the hallway side by side.

Katy's legs felt stiff, and she concentrated on moving gracefully. She wanted to relax and talk to Bryce as easily as Marlys did, but her breath came in little bursts and her heart thudded hard. It took all of her effort to walk and breathe. She couldn't find the ability to talk.

While she dug in her locker for her coat and the books she needed to take home, Bryce leaned against the next locker. "I wanted to tell you congratulations on being named the attendant for homecoming. That's a pretty big honor."

The heat from Katy's ears flooded to her cheeks. "Thanks. I was sure surprised."

He laughed, but not a mean laugh. "Bet so. I ... I guess that means you'll be there for the homecoming game? I mean, if you're an attendant, you kind of have to be there, right?" He laughed again, and this time it sounded self-conscious.

If it weren't for her spending the night with Shelby, she wouldn't be going. No matter if she was chosen as attendant or not, Dad probably would have told her no. He was always worried about her finding too much pleasure in activities away from Schellberg. *Honor thy father and mother*—the biblical admonition ran through her mind. "Yes, I'll be there."

A grin grew on his face. "Great. Then ..." She had everything she needed, so they started walking again. "Have you thought about being around all evening? I mean, for the whole game and not just the crowning ceremony?"

She'd thought of little else since yesterday at lunch. She shrugged, bunching her coat around her neck. "Kind of ..."

Bryce held the door open for her, and they stepped into the schoolyard. The bus waited by the curb. Katy needed to hurry, but she didn't want to leave Bryce until he'd asked her to homecoming. She looked at him, holding her breath.

"If you're going anyway, do you want to ... you know ... go with me? I mean, unless Michael asked you already ..."

Who was Michael? Then she remembered Michael Evans was the sophomore boy attendant. "Am I supposed to go with him?"

Bryce shook his head. The breeze picked up, and he snapped his jacket closed. "Not necessarily. Sometimes the attendants go to everything together, but ..."

Everything. Could "everything" mean the game *and* the dance? The bus driver blared the horn. "I have to go or ..." Katy started inching sideways along the walkway.

Bryce shoved his hands into his jacket pockets and followed. His heels scuffed on the pavement. "So ... do you want to ...?" He let the sentence dangle.

She reached the bus. "Yes." The word gasped out. She gulped and added, "I do." She nearly giggled. In two weeks, Dad would say "I do" to Mrs. Graber and his life would change forever. Would her life also change significantly since she'd uttered those words to Bryce? Even though it was a whimsical, romantic — almost silly — thought, she savored it anyway.

Bryce broke into a huge grin that made Katy's heart skip a beat. "Awesome! Well then, see you tomorrow, Katy."

Katy stood in place, watching him trot off.

"Kathleen, climb on," the bus driver chided. "We've got a schedule to keep."

"Sorry." Katy clambered on board. As she slipped past the bus driver, she said, "I'm going to homecoming. With Bryce." It felt good to say it out loud.

"Good for you. Sit down so we can get rolling."

Katy dropped her backpack on the closest seat and sat. The bus groaned away from the curb. Katy looked out the window, searching for Bryce. She spotted him in the parking lot beside his car. Her heart zinged when he looked up and waved. She waved back and then slumped down in the seat. She closed her eyes and hugged herself.

He'd asked her! He'd really asked her to homecoming! Thinking about it made her heart flutter more. Her feet might not know how to dance, but she felt like her heart might dance its way out of her chest while the bus tires rolled down the highway toward her stop.

Dad's pickup waited at the corner, and Katy dashed across the gravel. She climbed in quickly and gave the door an exuberant slam. "Hi, Dad!"

"Hi to you. You must have had a good day."

"Sure did."

He grinned. "Then maybe it's time for another driving lesson. Do you want to drive?"

"Yes!"

Dad got out and ran to the other side of the truck while Katy scooted across the seat. She settled herself behind the steering wheel. Dad hopped into the passenger seat. "Let's go."

With a little giggle, Katy put the truck into gear. She held tightly to the steering wheel with both hands as the truck bounced along the rutted road.

"I stopped by the grocer today and called Mr. Nuss."

Katy's heart skipped a beat. For the first time, it occurred to her that the Nusses might say no. Then everything would fall apart. "Is it okay if I stay with them the weekend after your wedding?"

"He said they'd be pleased to host you."

Katy slowed the truck as she turned a corner. Dust billowed outside her window, hiding the landscape from view for a moment.

"He also said there are some special events at the school that weekend and asked if it was all right for you to go with their family."

Katy sucked in a sharp breath, tasting dust from the road. Had Mr. Nuss told Dad about everything, including the fancy dress and the school dance? If Dad forbid her to go, she wouldn't disobey. But it would be very hard to tell Bryce she couldn't go after accepting his invitation.

"I said if you are staying with them, then you could do what their family did."

Katy let her air whoosh out. Obviously, Mr. Nuss hadn't mentioned all of the activities or Dad wouldn't be so agreeable. She pulled into their long driveway as Dad continued, "I trust the Nusses. And I trust you, Katy." He smiled at her. "At first I didn't want to go away and leave you by yourself. But I feel better now, knowing you'll be with Shelby and her family. They're good people."

Katy shut off the ignition and nibbled her lower lip. She should have been relieved. Nothing was standing in the way of going to the homecoming game and dance with Bryce. But Dad's approval didn't give her heart a lift. Instead, the happy flutters that had filled her chest from the moment Bryce had asked her came to an abrupt stop.

I trust you, Katy.

Dad's comment stung. She should tell him about being chosen as attendant, about needing a fancy dress, and about the dance. But when she opened her mouth, other words came out. "You and Mrs. Graber go, and don't worry about me. I'll be just fine."

Chapter Four

Katy deposited her backpack in her bedroom and changed into a work dress. Since she had an hour to spare before she needed to start supper, she plopped down at her desk and pulled out her journal. She wanted to record her memories of Bryce asking her to homecoming.

Words flew across the page. The writing looked a little shaky in places, evidence of her excitement, but she didn't let it bother her. She captured every emotion, every thought, every tiny detail. The memories filled two pages, front and back, and she paused before writing her conclusion.

> As exciting as it was to be asked, going to homecoming with Bryce is bound to be even better. He's so handsome and so nice. And he likes ME! I know I'm going to have a wonderful time. These next few days will be excruciatingly slow, but I intend to relish them and store up every look and smile Bryce and I exchange until the moment of our date arrives.

She sighed and closed her journal. She glanced at the little clock on her desk and gave a jolt. She needed to get started on supper! After closing the journal in her desk drawer, she clattered down the stairs to the kitchen.

Over the past weeks, she'd often come home and found Mrs. Graber and Gramma Ruthie at work in the kitchen, preparing casseroles and baked goods for the wedding celebration. She'd gotten a funny feeling in the pit of her stomach the first several times she saw Mrs. Graber at her stove or sink or table, but slowly Katy was getting used to the idea. Still, it was nice to have the kitchen to herself today — she could cook how she wanted to without Mrs. Graber offering to help or making suggestions for doing things differently.

Katy removed the big soup pot and a black iron skillet from the cabinet next to the stove. The stack of mismatched pots stirred an errant thought: *Mrs. Graber will probably bring her own pots, pans, and dishes when she marries Dad. She'll probably rearrange the cupboards too.* For a moment Katy squatted in front of the open cabinet door, memorizing the pile of familiar, dented, well-used items. *They're just pots. It's not a big deal.* She wasn't completely convinced, but she closed the door and placed the pot and skillet on the stove.

She dug in the refrigerator for the pork chops she'd asked Dad to bring up from the deep freeze the night before, then selected several potatoes from the bin right inside the cellar door. Dad wanted potatoes with every meal, but Katy hated going into the mildew-scented, spiderweb-filled cellar. So he'd put the bin at the top of the stairs for her. Katy appreciated his thoughtfulness.

She hummed while she peeled the potatoes, her eyes peeking out the window when a flock of birds swooped

through the yard or her horse, Shadow, galloped along
the fence. She smiled as Shadow tapped the ground with
one hoof, shaking her flowing black mane. Katy hoped
Shadow's baby looked just like its mama. Dad had mated
Shadow last summer, and the mare's stomach bulged with
the foal that would arrive sometime in late spring. As soon
as the colt was old enough, Katy intended to buggy-break
it and sell it. Since Shadow was her horse, Dad had promised she could have the money from the sale.

Although Katy hadn't shared her intentions yet with
Dad, she wanted to put the money into a fund for college
just in case the deacons approved her going on beyond
high school. Now that Dad would have Mrs. Graber, Katy
didn't need to worry about him being lonely when she
went away for good.

A car rolled into the yard, and Katy recognized Caleb
Penner's sedan. He was late today—Dad had been milking for close to an hour already. When Caleb hopped out of
his car, she instinctively leaned away from the window so
he wouldn't see her and wave. Why he thought she wanted
him waving to her, she couldn't guess, but if he saw her, he
always waved. She didn't want to greet him, and she avoided
the milking barn when he was there working with Dad.
She'd never met anyone who irritated her as much as Caleb.

She finished peeling the potatoes, put them on to boil,
then began mixing flour and seasonings to dredge the
pork chops. Just as she was dunking the first thick chop in
the flour mixture, someone tapped on the door. Her hands
sticky, she called, "It's open!"

The screen door squeaked, and Annika Gehring peeked
around the corner. Since only a mile's distance separated

their farms, Katy and Annika often walked to see one another. But with Katy attending high school in Salina, she and Annika hadn't had as much time together the past months. They had argued more than once about Katy's desire to go to school—Annika thought it was weird to continue school when Katy didn't have to—but even so, Katy missed seeing Annika every day. They'd been close friends since they were little girls.

She smiled. "Hi, Annika! Come on in."

"Let me take my shoes off first." Annika disappeared from view, and Katy heard scuffling noises. Annika's voice carried from around the corner. "It's still muddy in places from last week's melting snow, so my shoes are icky. I don't want to track mud across your floor."

Annika entered the kitchen, sliding a little bit as her socks met the smooth linoleum. She plopped a tinfoil-covered aluminum pan on the counter before crossing to the stove and peeking at what Katy was doing. "Mmm, pork chops." Annika smacked her lips. "Mom never fixes pork chops—Dad doesn't like them. The only pork we ever have is sausage."

Katy knew a hint when she heard one. Should she ask Annika to stay for supper? But her days with only her and Dad at the table would end soon. She decided to be selfish and not share her time with him. "The next time I fix them, I'll make sure I have extra." She hoped Annika wouldn't count the pork chops in the pan and wonder why two people needed four big chops. "Then you can join us."

Annika sighed. "Sounds good." She pointed to the container she'd brought in. "Mom sent over some apple turnovers. She wanted Mrs. Graber to try them in case she might want some for the wedding dinner." She looked around. "Is she here?"

"Not tonight." Katy carefully lowered the pork chops into the frying pan. They started to sizzle.

"I'm kind of surprised." Annika shifted aside as Katy reached to give the potatoes a stir with a long wooden spoon. "Isn't she pretty much here every night?"

Katy shrugged. "A lot, but not always." She headed to the cabinet to take down a can of peas. She dug in the drawer for the hand-operated can opener and clamped it onto the can. "I guess that'll change soon enough, though. Only two more weeks." *Two weeks from today, and I'll have a stepmother.* Her heart gave a little leap. *And then I'll have a date with Bryce.* Both events had the potential to bring permanent change into her life.

"Mom said your dad and Mrs. Graber are going to take a quick trip right after their wedding, back to Meschke to load up her remaining belongings."

Katy nodded. Everyone in Schellberg always knew everyone else's business. Sometimes it was comforting to live in such a close-knit community, where everybody knew her name and her family. But sometimes she wished they didn't know everything—like how her mother had left Katy, Dad, and the Mennonite faith. Katy didn't like living in Kathleen Jost Lambright's shadow. Maybe now that Dad was remarrying, people would forget about Katy's mom. *They might forget, but I won't.*

"Since you're going to be here by yourself, maybe I can come over and stay the nights while they're gone." Annika pulled out a small saucepan and held it out for

Katy to dump in the peas. "Wouldn't it be fun, having the whole house to ourselves?"

Katy put the pan of peas on the stove and adjusted the flame underneath it. "It would be fun, but ..." She offered a sorry look she didn't really feel. "Dad made arrangements for me to stay in Salina with Shelby and her family."

Annika's lips pinched together. Katy knew Annika was jealous of Shelby — Annika wanted Katy to herself. But Katy refused to give up her Salina friends. If she didn't have Shelby, Trisha, and Cora, she'd be totally alone at the school. *Except for Bryce* ...

Katy hurried on before Annika could argue. "Dad'll take me to meet the bus on Friday, then he and Mrs. Graber will leave for Meschke. I'll just go home with Shelby after school on Friday and stay until Monday. Then I'll be back Monday after school, like always."

"Except it won't be like always," Annika pointed out. "Because Mrs. Graber. I mean — " She giggled. "*Mrs. Lambright* will be here too. For good."

And after that weekend, Katy would know what it was like to have a date with a worldly boy. *To be like all the other teenage girls in the school* ... She mused, "That won't be the only thing that's changed." She hadn't really intended to say the thought out loud, but Annika perked up.

"What else is changing?"

The smell of scorched meat reached Katy's nose. She turned the pork chops quickly, grateful for the distraction. As much as she wished she could tell *someone*, Katy didn't dare tell Annika about homecoming. Annika would tell her mother, who would tell someone else, and eventually everyone from town would know. And they'd all disapprove. She searched for something that would make sense without giving away her plans.

"If I have a stepmother, she'll be doing a lot of the cooking and stuff that I've always done. I'll have a lot more free time."

Annika nodded, making the ribbons from her cap bounce. "I'm glad too. Maybe we'll get to spend more evenings together."

"I'll still have homework," Katy said, adjusting the flame under the pork chops since they were almost done. "But if I don't have to cook and clean up every night, we ought to have more time. Unless . . ." She sent Annika a sidelong glance, trying not to frown. "You end up spending more time with Caleb." If Annika was with Caleb, Katy would stay far, far away.

Annika sighed, lowering her head. She picked up the wooden spoon and slowly circled it through the pan of simmering peas. "I don't know if I'll be spending time with Caleb or not. I'd like to, but he's so shy."

Katy almost laughed. Caleb, *shy*?

"He just won't ask to keep company with me. And of course I can't ask him . . ."

Even though Katy didn't like Caleb, she did care about Annika. She hated to see her friend so sad. "Well, he's over here every day, helping out in the milking barn. So if you're around more, he'll see you more, and maybe he'll get enough nerve to, you know, ask to spend time with you."

Annika looked up, her eyes hopeful. "You think so?"

"Sure. The more you're together, the closer you're sure to grow." Katy thought about being in class with Bryce, going to forensics tournaments with Bryce, and attending homecoming with Bryce. Would they grow closer too? Should she even hope for such a thing, knowing Bryce wasn't Mennonite?

"I'd like that more than anything."

Caleb's mother had once told Katy that Caleb had a crush on her. If Caleb started paying more attention to Annika, Katy wouldn't have to worry about him anymore. She said, "Me too."

Annika gave Katy a quick hug. "You're a good friend, Katy." She scurried toward the door. "But you need to get your supper finished, so I'll get out of your way. I'll come back ... tomorrow after school?"

Katy turned off the fire underneath the skillet and both pans. "That'd be fine. Mrs. Graber might be here tomorrow and need my help, but I can still talk to you while we work."

"Or I'll help too, and we can finish early. Then maybe we can be ... I don't know ... hanging out in the barn or something when Caleb arrives." Annika's cheeks flushed pink.

Katy stifled a groan. Deliberately go where Caleb would be? But maybe it wouldn't be so bad, playing matchmaker for Annika and Caleb. At least Caleb wouldn't be pestering her anymore. Forcing a smile, Katy shrugged. "Sure. Why not?"

Annika left, and Katy drained the potatoes so she could mash them. Not until she was mounding the steaming, buttery potatoes into a serving bowl did she stop to think about something. Now that Shelby had a boyfriend, she spent more time with Jayden than with her girlfriends.

If Annika and Caleb started courting, Annika probably wouldn't be around Katy much anymore. With Dad getting married, he'd be focusing on his new wife instead of his daughter. A sad thought pinched her chest. Every person important to her seemed to be drifting away from her. Except one. *Bryce.*

The back door slammed. Dad clomped into the kitchen. He sniffed the air. "Mmm, Katy-girl, it smells good in here. Is supper ready?"

"I just need to make the gravy," Katy said. "Maybe five more minutes?"

"Good! I'll go up and change, and then we can eat." Dad headed around the corner. He called over his shoulder, "By the way, if it's not too late, you can go to the forensics meet this weekend if you want to. Rosemary said a couple of ladies have volunteered to help her and Gramma Ruthie, so they won't need you on Saturday."

Katy stared after her dad with her mouth hanging open. If she went to the tournament, she'd have another day with Bryce. Dad didn't know it, but he was playing matchmaker too.

Chapter Five

As they had for as far back as she could remember, Katy and Dad sat in the living room at the end of the day, and Dad read from the Bible. Katy loved their nightly reading time. The beauty of the old-world language in the Bible combined with the security of the routine always drew the day to a pleasant conclusion.

Dad opened his worn Bible and began reading from the fortieth chapter of Psalms. Katy closed her eyes and listened, Dad's deep voice as comforting as a lullaby. " 'I delight to do thy will, O my God: yea, thy law is within my heart ...' "

Katy's heart gave a jolt. Her eyes flew open. She knew the laws of her church fellowship. Dancing was not allowed. Going to the dance with Bryce would bring her delight, but was it against God's will for her? She heard Dad's voice in her head: *I trust you, Katy.*

Dad continued to read, and Katy rarely interrupted, but she couldn't keep her plans a secret for one more minute. She blurted, "Dad?"

Dad lifted his head, his brows pulled into a slight frown. "I'm not finished, Katy-girl."

"I know, but . . ." She swallowed. "I need to talk to you about something."

"Can't it wait?"

She shook her head.

Dad kept his finger on the spot where he'd left off reading. "All right then. What is it?"

"Mr. Nuss told you there was something special at school the weekend you and Mrs. Graber will be gone. You should know what it is." Katy explained homecoming. She told her dad how she'd been chosen as the sophomore attendant and what an honor it was. "And there's a dance after the game. A boy from my forensics class — he's a very nice boy, Dad. He comes to the morning Bible study group at school too. His name is Bryce . . ." Her mouth felt dry. She swallowed again. "He — Bryce — asked if I wanted to go to the game and the dance with him."

Katy watched her father's face. Dad's scowl didn't deepen, but the crease in his forehead didn't relax either. For a long while he sat looking at her but saying nothing. Katy held her breath until she thought her chest might explode. When would he speak?

Finally Dad cleared his throat. "Are you asking my permission to go to these things, Katy, or are you just telling me about it?"

Katy emptied her lungs with a whoosh. She bit down on her lower lip and thought for a moment. "I — I wanted you to know everything that was happening. You said I could do whatever the Nusses did, and I know Shelby is going to homecoming." Tears pricked her eyes. She wanted so badly to go with Bryce, to be with her Salina friends. "But I didn't want to hide it from you."

Dad slowly closed the Bible and laid it on the sofa cushion beside him. He still didn't smile. "I appreciate your telling me. Hiding things is never a good idea, because it leads to distrust."

Katy nodded miserably. She'd worked hard to regain Dad's trust after leaving school without permission with Jewel earlier in the year. Hearing him say he trusted her had been a gift. She didn't want to betray it. But, oh, how she wanted to go to homecoming with Bryce.

Dad smoothed his hand over the Bible cover. "There are many Scriptures in this book that I could quote right now. And if I started quoting them, I believe you could finish most of them. You've been taught well, and you know right from wrong."

Dad fell silent for a few moments, and Katy fidgeted under his serious gaze. Would he just hurry up and tell her she couldn't go and be done with it?

"You also know what the fellowship teaches — dancing can lead to immorality, which is a sin." Dad's cheeks flushed pink, but he maintained his steady eye contact with Katy. "And I think you know I believe indulging in worldly practices can't benefit your soul." Again he fell silent.

Katy stifled a sigh. "Dad, I — "

"But," Dad said as if Katy hadn't spoken, "I am going to honor what I told you earlier. I trust you. Which means I trust you'll make the right decision concerning what you do during your weekend with the Nusses."

Katy stared at Dad in confusion. He would let her

decide whether to attend homecoming? But he never let her decide on important things like this! "W-what?"

A smile—a sad one, Katy thought—tipped up the corners of Dad's lips. "You're growing up, and you need to start making decisions for yourself. That's not to say I don't want you coming to me to ask for advice or ask permission when new opportunities arise. I'm your father. I will always be involved in what you're doing, and while you live under my roof, you should respect my position of authority. But this time, I think you need to make your own choice. So you decide what to do, Katy-girl. Go to homecoming with Bryce, or not." He nodded, as if agreeing with himself that he'd advised her wisely. "I trust you to do the right thing."

Katy awakened early Saturday, even before her alarm clock rang. She'd hoped to go to the forensics tournament in Minneapolis, but Mr. Gorsky had turned in the list of contenders earlier in the week, and he couldn't change it. He'd been as disappointed as she, but there was nothing he could do—Katy couldn't compete. So instead she'd help Dad with the milking and then maybe work for Aunt Rebecca in her fabric shop in Schellberg since Mrs. Graber didn't need her help.

But not even the cows were awake yet. So Katy crept out of bed, snapped on her desk lamp, and pulled out her journal. She hadn't slept well the last two nights, thinking about whether to go to the dance. It would be simpler if her dad had just said yes or no. But he hadn't. Even so, she knew what he preferred. She had to decide: Do what Dad would have her do, or do what she wanted to do?

She flipped through her journal, seeking a poem she'd written a few months ago. It took awhile — the notebook pages were cluttered with words. But finally she located it, settled back, and read slowly.

> *So many feelings inside of me.*
> *I don't know ... who should I be:*
> *A girl who pleases everyone else*
> *Or one who only serves herself?*
> *My conscience bids me do what's right,*
> *But frankness begs to be given flight.*
> *Inside I long to rant and rage*
> *Against the rules that form my cage.*
> *But if I break from these restraints,*
> *Will I find freedom ... or merely pain?*

Katy knew what she wanted — to go to the dance with Bryce. She wanted the girls in her class who had snubbed her to see that she wasn't weird after all but just like them underneath her Mennonite cap and dress. She also knew what her dad wanted, and he didn't care about the girls in her class. He cared about his daughter pleasing God instead of men — or, in this case, high school students. She sighed, toying with the corner of the page. If she did what she wanted, knowing it would displease God, could she really be pleased with herself? That was the deepest dilemma.

She heard Dad's bedroom door creak open and his footsteps on the landing. He'd head down to the milking barn soon; she needed to dress and join him. She set aside her journal and put on one of her oldest dresses. While she and Dad saw to the cows, the sun made its appearance, promising a pleasant mid-February day. As she and Dad walked back to the house, Katy's thoughts drifted to Minneapolis, where the forensics team was probably unloading the bus.

"Rosemary, Gramma Ruthie, and a couple other ladies ought to be here soon," Dad said as they stepped into the kitchen and removed their dirty shoes. "A simple breakfast is fine. That way you won't have much cleaning up to do. Maybe just cereal and toast. Did you decide to — "

Katy sucked in a sharp breath. She wasn't ready to talk about the dance.

" — go in and help your aunt Rebecca today?"

Katy nearly collapsed with relief. She needed to make a decision about homecoming soon and let Dad know what she was doing, so she could quit worrying about it. "Yes, if you'll drive me in, I'll spend the day there. I'm sure she'll appreciate the help. I haven't been there much lately."

Dad nodded then headed for the stairs. "All right then. Let's get changed, eat, then I'll drive you to Schellberg. Might be Rosemary will have a shopping list for me too, and I can see to that while I'm in town."

Katy and Dad ate quickly, then Katy washed the dishes and Dad dried. Just as he placed the last clean bowl in the cupboard, they heard the crunch of tires in the yard. Dad reached the door in three wide strides and threw it open, letting in a rush of fresh-smelling air. Katy stood behind him and watched Mrs. Graber, Gramma, Mrs. Pankratz, and Mrs. Krehbiel cross the yard. Rosemary reached the house first, and Dad squeezed her hand as she stepped through the door.

"You ladies have a lot of work to do today?" The question was addressed to the group, but his eyes never left Mrs. Graber. Katy didn't know whether to giggle or roll her eyes at her dad's signs of infatuation.

Mrs. Graber sent Dad a crinkling smile. "We'll be getting the meat from the pork roasts and chickens we cooked last week ready to barbecue. We're using Mrs. Krehbiel's recipe, which everyone tells me is the best barbecue in the Midwest."

Dad nodded. "Everyone's right. Make plenty, then hopefully we'll have leftovers."

The ladies all laughed. Katy shook her head, marveling at her dad. He'd not been one to engage in idle chitchat or teasing comments before Mrs. Graber came along. As much as she enjoyed his more-relaxed side, she wondered why he couldn't have found it without Mrs. Graber's help.

Katy moved to Gramma Ruthie, and Gramma reached for a hug. Katy said, "Dad said you wouldn't need me, so I'm going to go work at Aunt Rebecca's." She released her grandmother but stayed close. "Are you going to drive me now, Dad?"

Dad said, "Sure. Rosemary, do you need anything from the stores in town?"

Rosemary shook her head, wrinkling her nose. "No, but we need you here. There are about two dozen roasts and just as many chickens in the trunk of my car. I hoped you might help us carry it in."

"Well, I can do that before I take Katy." Dad headed for the door. When he reached it, he paused and looked outside for a moment. He turned back and smiled. "Look here,

Katy—Caleb Penner's here. He probably wants his pay-check. Invite him in while I get my checkbook. He'll take his check to town to cash it like he always does, so see if he can take you to Rebecca's." He headed for the stairs.

Drive in with Caleb Penner? Katy scurried after her father. "Dad, I'm not in that big of a hurry. I can go later after you've carried in the meat."

Dad trotted up the stairs and called from the landing. "It would be silly for me to drive to Schellberg if Caleb's already going. Check to see if he's taking his check to town. If he is, ask if you can ride with him."

Katy couldn't disobey when Dad gave her a direction. Her only hope now was that Caleb wasn't planning to take his check to the bank right away.

Chapter Six

Caleb grinned ear to ear. "Sure, I'll be glad to give you a ride into town. I don't got anything else to do right now."

Oh, that boy's grammar! His improper speech always made Katy want to growl.

Caleb went on, unaware of Katy's irritation. "In fact, if your dad's gonna be busy, I can even pick you up after work and bring you on home again."

Before Dad could agree to the plan, Katy said, "That's all right. Just getting me there is fine. I'll get home another way."

Caleb stuck his hands in his jacket pockets and rocked on his boot heels. "You know, you should learn to drive. Then you could take yourself to town and back whenever you need to. You wouldn't have to bother other people."

Dad glanced up from the table where he was writing Caleb's check. "Is it a bother to take Katy to town, Caleb? If so, I can —"

"Oh, no!" Caleb's cheeks turned so red his freckles almost disappeared. "I didn't mean *I* thought she was a bother." He shot a sheepish grin in Katy's direction. "I was just saying . . ."

Dad nodded and looked back at the checkbook. He signed the check, tore it loose, and held it out to Caleb. "All right then. Thank you for your hard work, and thanks for giving Katy a ride this morning."

Caleb folded the check and slipped it into his shirt pocket. "No problem. And if you want, I could give her a driving lesson on the way into town."

Katy turned a horrified look on Dad.

Dad winked at Katy, letting her know he understood. "Well, thanks, but that's not necessary. I've been teaching Katy to drive. She knows how — we just don't have two vehicles. And I can't let her take the truck in case I need it."

Mrs. Graber turned from the cabinet, where she'd been removing the roasting pans. "Samuel, it's all right with me if Katy takes my car into town." She laughed softly. "After you've taken all the meat out of the trunk, of course."

Katy stared at Mrs. Graber in surprise. She'd really let Katy borrow her car?

But Dad shook his head. "Thank you, but we'd better keep your car here. I can't transport all of the ladies in my truck if they'd need to leave before Katy returns. Besides, I haven't had time to take her to Salina to get her license yet. I don't mind her driving my truck on the back roads, but I don't think I should let her drive your car into town without a license."

"I suppose that's wise." Mrs. Graber offered Katy an *I'm sorry* look. Then she said, "Maybe when we get back from our trip, I can take Kathleen to the driver's license bureau and let her take the driving test."

Dad said, "Sounds like a good plan." Mrs. Graber and Dad exchanged a tender look, and then she turned her attention back to the pans in the cupboard.

Caleb furrowed his forehead as if in deep thought. "If Katy's gonna start driving, you might start askin' around in town to see if anybody's got a car they're willing to sell. Or call the auto dealership in McPherson — the one on the highway. They've been real good about findin' cars for Dad that meet the fellowship's approval."

Katy nearly rolled her eyes. Who was Caleb Penner to butt into their family business and give Dad advice? Didn't he know how ridiculous he looked, trying to be all grown up?

Dad smoothed his fingers over his mouth, removing his grin. "Thanks, I'll keep that in mind. Now ..." He nodded toward the back door. "Don't you think you'd better get Katy to town? Her aunt's store opens in less than fifteen minutes."

"Oh! Yeah — sure." Caleb whirled and thumped toward the door. "C'mon, Katy. You don't wanna be late." His tone held an admonishment.

And just who has been holding us up? Not me! Katy wished she could glare at Dad for making her go with Caleb, but she just followed Caleb across the yard and climbed into the passenger seat of his sedan. *Only a five-minute ride into Schellberg. I can tolerate Caleb Penner for five minutes.*

Caleb pulled onto the road, shooting her a grin. "Purty today, ain't it?"

Katy ground her teeth together. She managed to squeeze out, "Mm-hmm."

"S'posed to stay nice all next week too."

Caleb drove with one hand on the steering wheel and one arm propped on the window frame. Dad had told Katy to keep both hands on the wheel in case they hit a pothole or an animal ran out of the ditch. She started to tell Caleb so, but he spoke again.

"Y'know, your dad's getting married on the twenty-fifth — "

As if she wouldn't know that!

" — an' then him an' your stepmom are going away for the weekend, right?"

She had no idea why he needed to confirm her dad's plans, but she nodded.

"You stayin' by yourself at the farm?"

Katy frowned at Caleb. What was he after? "No."

His eyebrows shot up. "Oh yeah? Stayin' with Annika then?"

"No."

"Oh ..." A smug grin formed on his freckled face. "With your grandparents, right?"

For some reason, it gave Katy pleasure to reply, "No."

He grunted. "Then your aunt and uncle?"

She swallowed an amused giggle. "Huh-uh."

Caleb shot her a frustrated look. "Who're you stayin' with?"

Her plans were none of Caleb Penner's concern. Katy shrugged. "No one you know."

For the next mile, Caleb sat in silence, his lips twitching as if he'd captured a bumblebee in his mouth and it was trying to escape. Finally he said, "But you'll be close by, won't you?"

He is the most persistent person. Katy sighed. "Why does it matter?"

Red climbed from Caleb's jaw to his cheekbones. "Well, Julie and Jerome Pankratz are hosting a singing at their place the Saturday after your dad's wedding. I thought maybe you'd want to, I dunno, go with me."

Oh, I'm so glad I won't be here. "Sorry, Caleb, but that won't work for me," Katy said. She hoped she didn't sound as relieved as she felt. "Why don't you ask Annika? She loves to sing." *And she likes you, although I can't figure out why.*

"Antarctica?" He used the nickname he'd chosen for Annika when they were still in grade school. At least he'd stopped calling Katy *Katydid*. She didn't miss the silly nickname at all. "I guess I could ask her, but—"

He made the turn toward town, a little faster than Dad had taught her to make turns. Katy steadied herself by bracing both hands on the dash.

Caleb added, "Asking Annika would prob'ly give her ideas."

"And what's wrong with that?"

He made a face. "C'mon, Katy ..."

Protectiveness welled up inside of Katy. Annika liked Caleb—really liked him—and he was being mean. Shifting slightly on the seat so she could face him, she folded her arms over her chest. "No, really. What would be so wrong with spending time with Annika? She's a nice girl, and—" She couldn't tell Caleb Annika liked him. It would betray a confidence, and Annika would be mortified. She finished, "—she's a lot of fun to be around."

"She's bossy. And she laughs like a hyena."

Katy wanted to argue, but she had to admit Annika's shrill giggle whenever Caleb was around had annoyed her too. But Annika only did it out of nervousness. "But—"

Caleb shook his head. "Nah, I don't want to take Annika. I want to take you."

"Well, you can't." Katy didn't mean to sound so abrupt. She softened her tone. "I won't be in town that weekend. So if you don't want to take Annika, I guess you'll have to go by yourself."

They reached Schellberg, and Caleb drove straight to Aunt Rebecca's shop on the north end of Main Street. He pulled up to the curb, put the gearshift into park, but left the engine running. Then he looked at Katy. His lips poked into a pout that wasn't at all attractive. "Well, if not the singing at the Pankratz's, then what about—"

"Caleb."

Caleb stopped talking, but he left his mouth hanging open. It was all Katy could do to keep from reaching across the seat and closing it with a nudge on his chin.

"I appreciate the invitation. It's very nice of you to ask me." *Irritating but nice.* "But to be perfectly honest, I'm not interested in going to parties with you. You said asking Annika would give her ideas. Well, my going with you might give *you* ideas. And I don't want to mislead you."

"So you're saying you still don't like me."

Maybe he was smarter than she'd given him credit for being. Katy sighed. "Not like that." She started to apologize, but she realized she wasn't really sorry. So she held the words inside.

He glared out the window, his fist clamping and unclamping on the steering wheel. "All right. That's fine then." He sounded angry. And hurt.

Even though Katy didn't particularly care for Caleb, she hadn't intended to hurt his feelings. She said, "Caleb, I — "

"Don't you need to get to work?"

She drew back, startled by his chilly tone. Although he wasn't exactly a polite person, he'd never spoken so rudely to her before. She nodded.

"Then go on. I've got things to do."

Katy opened the door and started to step out. But before she could slide out of the seat, Caleb grabbed her elbow. She looked at him in surprise.

"You know, Katy, there's only one boy in town interested in you. Me. With all your weird ideas about school an' stuff, none of the other unmarried guys want anything to do with you. They think you're pretty enough, but they all say you're stuck on yourself."

Katy's ears flamed. Stuck on herself? In the Mennonite community, there were few insults worse than being called self-important. She started to protest, but Caleb went on.

"Your dad's teaching me to be a dairyman, and he tells me all the time I'm doin' a good job for him. I'm pretty sure he would say yes if I asked permission to start courting you. Seein' as how nobody else wants to court you and your dad likes me, you might want to think again about telling me no."

Katy pulled her arm from Caleb's grasp. "I'm not going to be here that weekend, Caleb. I already told you that." Now she was happier than ever that she wouldn't be in town that weekend. If she were here, Annika would talk her into going to the singing. She couldn't possibly go to a party with the young people, since she knew what they thought about her.

"But you won't be gone every weekend. There'll be other parties."

Caleb was right. With spring around the corner, the young people would be getting together nearly every weekend for singings, popcorn parties, or volleyball games. Boys and girls would start pairing up, as they did every spring. Although Katy wasn't ready to begin courting, she'd eventually want to marry and have a family. What would she do if none of the boys in Schellberg wanted to court her — *ever*?

Caleb revved the engine. The car shuddered in place, sending a shiver down Katy's spine. "I guess since you aren't going to be staying in Schellberg the weekend of your dad's wedding, you must be staying with one of your Salina friends."

Katy didn't answer.

Caleb made a little snort — a snide sound. "Kinda figured when you started going to that school, they'd end up pulling you away from Schellberg. Well, if you're that easily drawn in by the world, I probably wouldn't want to court you anyway." He jabbed his thumb against his chest. "I intend to stay in the church."

"So do I!"

"Yeah, right."

Katy glared at Caleb. "You don't know anything about me, the school, or the people there, Caleb, so don't you dare be derisive and arrogant!"

Caleb's eyes narrowed. "And don't you dare be so smart all the time." His lips formed a mocking smirk. "All your fancy words and your high school classes — you think you're making me look stupid, but you're wrong. You're just making yourself look like a fool."

Katy jumped out of the car and slammed the door as hard as she could. To her chagrin, the slam didn't break the window. Shattering the glass would have given her great satisfaction at that moment. She charged onto the sidewalk as Caleb's car squealed away from the curb, stirring up dust. Coughing, she stumbled toward Aunt Rebecca's shop and flung open the door with force, making the little bell hanging above it clang angrily.

Aunt Rebecca popped up from behind the cutting counter and stared at Katy with disapproval. "Katy! What do you think you are — " But when Katy burst into tears, her aunt cut her reprimand short.

Chapter Seven

Aunt Rebecca flew around the counter, the black ribbons of her cap waving over her shoulders as if caught in a stout breeze. "What is it? Did something happen to Samuel?"

Katy was crying too hard to answer.

Aunt Rebecca grabbed Katy's shoulders and gave her a little shake. "What is it? What's wrong?"

Katy drew in several shuddering breaths and choked out, "Caleb says e-everyone thinks I'm—I'm stuck on myself!"

Aunt Rebecca dropped her hands and stepped back. Her brows pinched into a frown. "Is *that* what all these tears are about? Honestly, Katy." She released a mighty breath, shaking her head. She took a handkerchief from her pocket and pressed it into Katy's hand. "Stop crying, and blow your nose. You need to save your tears for the big hurts."

Katy wanted to tell her aunt this *was* a big hurt. How humiliating to know the young people in town had called her self-important behind her back. Her chest ached with the effort of containing the pain inflicted by Caleb's taunt. But she obediently wiped her eyes, blew her nose, and pushed the crumpled handkerchief into her own pocket for washing later.

Aunt Rebecca put her hands on her hips and gave Katy a no-nonsense look. "Now tell me what happened with Caleb."

Katy would have preferred to drop the subject given her aunt's lack of compassion. Aunt Rebecca had never been very warm and affectionate—not even with her own children. Dad said she couldn't take time for tenderness because she had too many responsibilities. But Katy didn't think that was a good excuse. Gramma Ruthie, Mrs. Penner, and Mrs. Graber were also very busy women, but they always had time for kindness.

"Katy?" Aunt Rebecca tipped her head and peered into Katy's face. She wouldn't let up until Katy answered her questions.

Katy sighed. She abbreviated the exchange as best she could. "Caleb asked me to go to the singing at the Pankratz place the Saturday after Dad and Mrs. Graber get married. I told him I couldn't go because I won't be in town. He asked if I'd go to other singings with him, and I told him I didn't think I should because I don't like him that way. Then he got mad and told me I should go with him because no other boys would ask since they— they—" Tears tightened her throat, and she swallowed. "They all think I'm stuck on myself."

"And why would they think that?"

Katy hugged herself, her chest aching. "Caleb said it's because I use big words when I talk. And because I go to high school."

Her aunt nodded. "Yes, I can see that."

Before she started crying again, Katy spun away from Aunt Rebecca. Aunt Rebecca took hold of Katy's shoulders and tried to turn her around. Katy resisted. She did *not* want to look at Aunt Rebecca right now! But her aunt's hands tugged harder, and Katy had no choice. To her surprise, instead of her customary stern look, Aunt Rebecca's face reflected sympathy.

"Katy, I didn't mean *I* thought you were self-important. I can see, based on what Caleb said, why the young people might think so, though."

"Just because I like words? And learning? That isn't fair." Katy sputtered the protest, still battling back tears. "Annika likes cooking, and she tells everyone how good her new recipes taste. Caleb likes fixing car engines and is always bragging about how he keeps his old sedan running even though it's got over two hundred thousand miles on it. I don't show off about going to school—I just go. So why am I the self-important one?"

"Because it's so different from what everyone else has done," Aunt Rebecca answered calmly. She put her hands on her hips again. "Have you considered that Caleb and some of the others might be jealous?"

Katy blinked twice. "J-jealous?"

Aunt Rebecca nodded. "Yes. You were given a special opportunity. You're getting to see and experience things the others aren't. That could very well create jealousy."

Katy contemplated her aunt's suggestion. Their fellowship encouraged members to live simply and stay within certain boundaries in regard to what they owned so they wouldn't cause their neighbor to covet. Even so, Katy was aware that some families without electricity—such as

Annika's — at times looked with envy at the families who did have electricity. Annika often asked to spend summer nights at Katy's house because Katy had an electric fan that stirred the air to help cool things down.

When the deacons discussed Katy's request to attend public high school, one of their biggest concerns was whether it would create dissension in the community, with other young people feeling as though Katy was being given an unfair advantage. Because of the deacons' concerns, she didn't talk about school at the young people's gatherings. So she didn't believe she deserved their criticism.

Katy said, "Being jealous doesn't give them the right to talk about me behind my back." Hurt rose again as she thought about the others discussing her, calling her names, maybe even laughing at her. Her voice croaked as she added, "We're supposed to go to the person who offends us and talk directly to them. Nobody's done that."

"Caleb did," Aunt Rebecca said.

Yes, Caleb sure did. And Katy hadn't appreciated it at all. She frowned and folded her arms tightly over her chest. "But he didn't do it *lovingly*."

To Katy's surprise, Aunt Rebecca laughed. "Oh, Katy." She shook her head, her eyes twinkling. "Boys Caleb's age haven't learned to be tactful. They just blurt things out. Especially when their egos are bruised, they can be hurtful."

Katy nodded. For once, Aunt Rebecca was absolutely right. She'd given Caleb's ego a big punch by refusing to go to the singing with him. And she was certain if she asked Caleb to define the word *tact*, he'd just stare at her with his mouth hanging open. She pictured it, and despite her feelings a little bubble of laughter formed in the back of her throat.

Aunt Rebecca guided Katy to the coat pegs at the back of the store. "Even though Caleb didn't go about it the right way, maybe it's good you know how the young people feel. Being at peace with the members of the fellowship is important. Now that you know there is a concern, you can pray about the best way to address it."

Katy paused in removing her coat. Her eyes flew wide. "Why should *I* address it? I'm not the one with the problem — they are. *They* were wrong to make assumptions about me and" — she searched for what Caleb would term a fancy word — "malign my character."

Aunt Rebecca pursed her lips, no doubt disapproving of the rebellion in Katy's voice. "What does it say in Proverbs nineteen, verse eleven?"

Katy pressed her memory, but she couldn't retrieve the verse.

Aunt Rebecca quoted, " 'The discretion of a man defereth his anger; and it is his glory to pass over a transgression.' " She looked directly into Katy's eyes, and her usual bossy tone emerged. "You have no control over anyone's behavior but your own. Getting angry will distance you further from the young people in the fellowship. Is that what you want?"

At that moment Katy wanted to be as far as possible from Caleb and the others, but deep down she knew the reason their comments hurt so much was because she desired to be a part of their circle of friendship. She shook her head slowly.

Aunt Rebecca sighed. "As hard as it might be for you,

someone must take the steps needed to restore peace. It would be to your glory to pass over the transgression and work to make things right again."

The little bell above the door *ting-a-linged*, signaling the arrival of a customer. Aunt Rebecca leaned forward and whispered, "You pray for the opportunity to speak with the young people, Katy, and I'll pray they are receptive." Then she whirled around and bustled over to the customer. "Mrs. Gebhardt! Good morning. What can I do for you today?"

Katy placed her coat on a peg and then slipped through the curtained doorway into the storage area in back of of Aunt Rebecca's shop. She climbed onto one of the tall stools next to the sorting table and rested her chin in her hand. *Self-important.* The title stung. *But could it be even a tiny bit accurate?*

Katy didn't want to validate Caleb's accusation, but she thought about her excitement over being chosen the sophomore attendant above all the other girls in her class. Even though she still wondered why the seniors had picked her—they'd never paid attention to her before—she relished the honor. She thought about how it made her feel—important and accepted—when Bryce asked her to go to the homecoming dance. Then she thought about forensics and how much she wanted to win medals at the competitions. Her conscience twinged. Was it possible school happenings were giving her a sense of self-importance?

Her whole life, she'd been taught that serving God first was the only way to find true contentment. She'd truly believed going to high school was an answer to prayer, and the deacons wouldn't have approved it if they'd thought it

was against God's will. But somehow she needed to figure out if the things she was doing at the school—all of
the things, from learning in the classes to participating in
extra activities—were pleasing to God. She had much to
think about.

"Katy?" Aunt Rebecca called from the front of the store.

Katy jumped off the stool and peeked through the doorway into the display area. "Yes?"

Aunt Rebecca pointed to Mrs. Penner and Mrs. Tieszen,
who waited by the cutting table. "Would you help them,
please?"

Even though Mrs. Penner was Caleb's mother, Katy
liked the woman. Caleb resembled his mom with his red
hair and freckles, but most of time he didn't act like her.
Mrs. Penner was one of the nicest people Katy knew. How
had she ended up with a son like Caleb? Katy flashed a
smile and moved quickly to the table. "I'd be glad to."

Mrs. Penner placed a bolt of ecru cotton strewn with
tiny green ivy vines on the table. "Five and a half yards,
please."

Katy set to work measuring the fabric.

Mrs. Penner fiddled with a spool of thread while she
watched. "It's good to see you, Katy. No forensics tournament today?"

Katy flipped the bolt several times, freeing more fabric.
"There's one in Minneapolis today, but I thought I might
be helping Mrs. Graber with wedding preparations, so I
didn't sign up to go."

"Oh, that's too bad. I know you enjoy competing, and
I've heard you do very well."

Katy sent her a quick look—could Mrs. Penner think

Katy had been boasting about her accomplishments? But she smiled sweetly. Katy swallowed a relieved sigh. "Thank you. I do enjoy it, and my teacher has been very encouraging."

"That's nice."

Mrs. Tieszen stood listening to their conversation, her eyes looking round and owlish behind her thick glasses. "So you'll continue on at that school after this year?"

Katy had only been given permission for her sophomore year, even though she hoped to go all the way through to earn her high school diploma, and maybe go to college. But after her conversations with Aunt Rebecca and Caleb, she needed to do some deep soul-searching. Dad had told her he trusted her to make the right decisions, but she knew she'd need help in choosing the right thing.

She answered carefully. "I'm praying about what is best for me." *About next year, and this year's homecoming activities.*

Mrs. Tieszen nodded, satisfied. Mrs. Penner beamed in approval. And from across the room, Aunt Rebecca looked up and smiled. Their responses to her statement warmed her and let her know she was on the right track. *God, I'll be asking. Please give me answers I can understand — and accept.*

Chapter Eight

The morning passed quickly with lots of activity and shoppers. Aunt Rebecca finally released Katy at one o'clock to run next door to the little café to eat a hamburger for lunch. When she'd finished eating, she ordered an extra one and took it to Aunt Rebecca. Aunt Rebecca accepted it with a grateful, tired smile.

"Thank you. I haven't had a single soul come in since you left. Maybe we can hope for a quiet afternoon. After our busy morning, we've earned it." She sank onto a stool and unwrapped her hamburger. Bowing her head, she prayed, and then looked at Katy. "While I'm eating, would you mind straightening the fabric bolts on the back shelves? Mrs. Tieszen, bless her heart, has such a hard time seeing the information printed on the ends of the bolts, she has to pull everything askew. The whole shelf is a mess."

Remembering the woman's thick glasses, Katy nodded. "Sure, I can do that."

She scurried to the back wall of the shop, where built-in shelves reached from the floor to the ceiling. Each shelf held bolts of colorful fabric, which were usually standing upright like soldiers on parade. Katy rounded the corner and slapped her hand to her cheek in dismay. Half of the bolts had been pulled out and laid flat in haphazard stacks. The others were flopped sideways, leaning like a dilapidated fence after a windstorm. Calicos were mixed with paisleys, and two bolts of gingham had been moved from the top shelf to the bottom one. How could one woman make such a mess? Katy pressed her memory, trying to recall what Mrs. Tieszen had purchased. She snickered when she remembered. *All this rearranging for a quarter yard of plain blue cotton.*

With a sigh, Katy set to work. An hour and forty-five minutes later, she brushed her hands together and smiled in satisfaction at the neatly organized shelves. When she turned to go ask her aunt what she could do next, her gaze fell on a bolt of fabric resting on the windowsill. With the sun streaming across it, the lavender fabric seemed to shimmer. Katy gasped in pleasure. She scooped up the bolt and smoothed her hand over the slightly stiff, sheeny fabric. She'd thought her purple tone-on-tone dress was made of the prettiest fabric she'd ever seen, but this lavender material was even lovelier.

Aunt Rebecca walked over and plucked the bolt from Katy's hands. "Don't put this on the shelves. I set it aside because I'm going to return it."

Katy gawked at her aunt. "Why?"

Aunt Rebecca gawked back. "*Why?* Look at it, Katy!"

Katy looked. "What's wrong with it?" The fabric appeared flawless, the smooth fabric such a delightful color. She imagined fairy princesses wore gowns of fabric like this.

Aunt Rebecca clicked her tongue on her teeth. "It's organdy. None of the ladies in our fellowship would make a dress from organdy—too sheer." She wrinkled her nose. "Organdy is fine for curtains or aprons, but can you imagine anyone hanging something that like in their kitchen window? It's just too ... gaudy."

Katy gazed at the fabric. "It's *never* used for dresses?"

Aunt Rebecca tapped her lips with her finger. "Well, yes, I suppose for specialty dresses—as an overlay for a silk or lightweight matelassé." She dropped the bolt into Katy's arms. "But it just isn't practical. I must have written down the wrong number on my last order and received it by mistake. It needs to go back to the factory. So package it in some of that mailing paper in the storeroom and address it for me, would you? The factory's address is on the pad beside the cash register."

"All right." Katy's tennis-shoe heels scuffed as she moved to obey her aunt. She spread heavy brown paper across the work table then laid the bolt on the paper. The lavender against the plain brown made the fabric appear even more beautiful. *Cora and Trisha said all the girls wore beautiful gowns to the homecoming dance. Maybe I could use this fabric to sew a dress.* She drew squiggles on the fabric with her finger, imagining how she might look in the soft, shimmering lavender.

The sewing machine set up in the front window of the shop began to hum. Aunt Rebecca must be working on a project. Katy stared at the curtained doorway separating the shop from the storage area, her hands idle. She bit her lower lip. Aunt Rebecca expected her to prepare this fabric for return to the factory, and she should follow her directions. Aunt Rebecca *was* the boss. But if this fabric went back, Katy wouldn't have the opportunity to use it — if she decided to go to the homecoming dance.

She dashed to the doorway and threw the curtain aside. "Aunt Rebecca?"

Aunt Rebecca lifted her foot, silencing the machine. "What is it?"

"This organdy . . . could you maybe hold onto it a little longer?"

Her aunt scowled. "Katy, I told you — it isn't practical. No one — "

"I might have a use for it. But I'm not sure yet. So could you wait until I know for sure?"

"When will you know?"

Katy drew in a breath and held it. Homecoming was only two weeks away. "Soon."

Aunt Rebecca pushed the machine treadle. She raised her voice over the hum of the motor. "There's a two-week return policy, and it came in yesterday. So it has to be postmarked by February twenty-sixth."

The day of the dance. "I'll know before then."

"All right, Katy. Set it aside then, and start vacuuming. I think I'll be able to send you home early today."

"Thank you!" Katy whisked the curtain back into place and trotted to the table. She scooped up the fabric and held it to her beating heart. Closing her eyes, she envisioned herself gliding around the dance floor with Bryce, the lights in the gym making the lavender fabric shimmer. She heaved a huge sigh followed by a little giggle. Then she set the bolt on a shelf in the corner of the storeroom and headed to the closet for the vacuum cleaner.

On Sunday after worship services, Gramma Ruthie invited Katy and Dad for lunch. She also invited Annika, and Annika eagerly accepted the invitation. Katy had never known Annika to refuse the opportunity to eat at someone else's house. Annika did much of the cooking and cleaning up in her own home and complained about it. But guests weren't expected to clean up, so Annika enjoyed being a guest. Katy wondered if Annika would ask people to her home for meals when she married and started a family of her own.

"Do you know what your grandma's making for lunch?" Annika asked as the girls walked to the row of vehicles lined up on the sunny side of the church yard. "I hope she made a pot roast. Hers is always more tender than anyone else's."

Katy laughed. "Dad would say that's because he butchered the beef."

Annika rolled her eyes. "Of course a man who never does the cooking would try to take the credit." But she grinned, so Katy knew she was joking.

The girls leaned against the hood of Dad's truck and waited for the grown-ups to end their conversations and head for home. Even though it was February and supposedly winter, the past two days had proven mild and sunny. No one seemed in a hurry to leave the churchyard. Across the yard, Aunt Rebecca and Uncle Albert visited with Caleb's parents. Katy smiled, thinking of how Aunt Rebecca had spoken to her like an adult rather than a child when she'd been so upset yesterday. Even though Aunt

Rebecca hadn't hugged Katy, she'd spoken kindly. And Katy knew her aunt would follow through on her promise to pray for her.

Remembering Aunt Rebecca's promise to pray reminded her what Caleb had said. Whirling toward Annika, she grabbed her friend's arm. "Annika, I have to ask you something."

Annika shifted and gave Katy her attention.

"Have you heard the young people talk about me? At parties or singings?"

Annika frowned. "Talk about you? How?"

"Calling me names, like stuck-up or — " Katy tried to think of a term Caleb would use. She said, "Smart aleck. Anything like that?"

Annika squirmed. "Why do you want to know?"

The hesitant reply confirmed Katy's fears. She cringed. "Do I really act that way?"

Annika looked down and rubbed the toe of her shoe over the flat, brown grass. "Not on purpose, I don't think. But sometimes, well ..." Annika scrunched her face and peeked at Katy. "It's just that you're different. The way you say things. Probably because you're always reading. You use words other people wouldn't. It makes you seem kind of ... weird."

How Katy hated that word! She pressed, "But the others didn't call me weird — they called me stuck-up?"

"Only a couple of the guys," Annika said. She grabbed Katy's hand. "But don't let it bother you. They aren't worth worrying about." She glanced around, then turned back to Katy. "How'd you find out? I mean, did someone actually call you stuck-up to your face?"

Katy nodded. "Caleb did."

Annika's jaw dropped. "He didn't!"

"He did. And he told me everyone else thought I was stuck on myself too."

Annika cupped her hand over her eyes and searched the church grounds. "Where is he?"

Katy grabbed her arm. "Annika—"

Annika shook loose. "No! I'm going to let him know how rude he was. He shouldn't have said that to you."

"Yes, he should have."

Annika stared at Katy in surprise.

"I needed to know." Katy's statement even surprised herself. She wouldn't have ever thought she'd defend Caleb. "But," she added, "he shouldn't have said it the way he did—he was mad at the time."

"Why was he mad?"

Katy's ears started to heat up. "It doesn't matter. I'd irritated him, and he retaliated by telling me I was stuck on myself. Even though I didn't like hearing it, maybe it was good I did. It's—it's made me stop and think about some things and whether I should change them."

Annika leaned close, her eyes flashing. "You mean you're thinking about not going to school anymore? Because if you stayed home, then—"

"No, not that," Katy said before Annika could get all excited. "I'm going to finish the year. But there are some things going on at school that I'm involved in. I might not participate after all." Her heart panged. Being chosen as the attendant was such an honor—an honor she wanted to accept. But not if it would make her self-important. Even though she'd prayed hard about it the night before, God hadn't answered yet. She hoped He'd hurry up. She needed to let Aunt Rebecca know about that fabric.

"What is it?" Annika asked.

"I don't want to talk about it." Katy offered a sorry look that she hoped Annika would accept. "It won't matter if I don't do it. But if I do go ahead with it, you'll be the first to know." *After Dad, of course.*

Annika looked disappointed, but for once she didn't argue. Before the girls could talk anymore, Gramma Ruthie and Grampa Ben approached. Katy sucked on her lower lip as she watched them walk slowly across the grass, arm in arm. She loved them so much; she couldn't imagine what it would be like when they weren't around anymore. If she decided to be the homecoming attendant, maybe her grandparents would come to watch her. Dad and Mrs. Graber would be away on their trip, but it would be nice to have some family there. Maybe she'd even invite Aunt Rebecca, Uncle Albert, and her cousins. The twins, Lola and Lori, would be green with envy to see Katy out on the gym floor with the other attendants! And Annika could come too. Katy would have a whole cheering section. The thought made her smile.

But then her smile faded. What was she thinking, putting together a cheering section and trying to make her cousins jealous? Only a truly self-centered person would want to show off for her family and friends. Caleb's jibe echoed through her mind: *You're stuck on yourself. You're stuck on yourself.*

Gramma Ruthie cupped Katy's cheek when she reached the truck. "There's my sweet girl."

Katy's stomach swirled. Gramma wouldn't call her "sweet" if she knew what kinds of thoughts entered Katy's head. She forced herself to smile.

"Rosemary is riding with your dad," Gramma said, "so he said you and Annika should go with us. Are you ready?"

"I'm ready."

"Me too," Annika said.

They followed Grampa Ben to his car. He opened the back door and bowed, sweeping his hand in an invitation for the girls to climb in. "Let's go."

Annika giggled as she slipped into the seat, but Katy got in silently. Her grandparents chatted as Grampa drove, their soft voices an accompaniment to the grit of tires on gravel. The familiar routine—worship, dinner with her grandparents, visiting—should have blanketed Katy in comfort. But today she had to continually blink, an attempt to control unsettling tears that pressed for release.

Annika bumped her with her elbow and whispered, "Are you okay?"

Katy looked out the window and didn't answer. She wasn't okay. She wouldn't be okay until she'd finally made a decision about homecoming. Why hadn't Dad decided for her? Letting her be grown up and choose for herself was proving to be too hard.

Chapter Nine

Jewel stared at Katy. "You can't be serious." Cora and Trisha exchanged looks. Katy held her hands out in a gesture of *what?* Jewel snorted, rolled her eyes, and turned to Cora and Trisha. "She's serious."

Katy leaned against the school's brick exterior and folded her arms over her chest. Yesterday's sunny sky had disappeared under a cloak of gray clouds. She wished the bell would ring so they could go inside. She also wished Shelby would join them instead of hanging out with Jayden and his friends. Somehow Shelby always understood Katy better than Cora, Trisha, or especially Jewel. Shelby would listen and see Katy's reasons for declining the opportunity to be the sophomore class homecoming attendant.

Katy said, "If I can't do it, they'll just choose someone else, right? I mean, if the seniors voted for the attendants, there's got to be a second-place girl."

Jewel huffed. A little cloud of condensation hung in front of her face for a few seconds and then whisked away on the breeze. "Yeah, but who'd want to be recognized as the *second-place* girl? There's no glory in being runner-up." Jewel scowled. "Especially runner-up to *you*. I mean, who knows why they picked the weird little Amish girl in the first place, but no way would anyone want to do it knowing it was only 'cause you turned it down."

"Jewel, don't be mean," Trisha chided. She turned to Katy. She looked worried. "I think Jewel's right. It would be so, like, embarrassing to even do it knowing you got it by default."

Cora hugged herself and bounced in place. "The thing is, if you turn it down, the sophomore class won't be represented. So if you tell the principal you can't be the attendant, they'll probably just have Michael stand up there by himself."

"And wouldn't *that* look stupid."

Katy cringed at Jewel's derisive tone.

Jewel pulled the furry collar of her coat up around her jaw and glared at Katy. "Look, Miss Has-To-Be-Difficult, if you back out, you're proving everybody in the school right—that you're just a weird girl who doesn't belong."

Katy hung her head. Her chest felt tight and achy. She hoped she wouldn't cry.

"Jewel!" Trisha stared at the other girl in open-mouthed disbelief. "That's the meanest thing you've ever said!"

Jewel shrugged. "I'm just speaking truth, girlfriend." She looked skyward and flipped her hands outward, as if petitioning the heavens. "Boggles the mind that they even chose her. It's gotta be some big colossal joke." She whirled on Katy, giving her a squinty-eyed look. "But if you turn it down? Big mistake. *Big* mistake." Jewel stomped off, her long hair—dyed reddish-purple this week—swinging.

Cora scuttled close to Katy. "Don't let her bother you. You know when she gets in a bad mood, she takes it out on anybody around."

Katy glared at Jewel's retreating back. "Well, I've had about enough of her dissing *me*."

Trisha and Cora burst out laughing.

Katy turned her glare on them.

They laughed harder.

Katy started to walk off, but Trisha grabbed her arm and held her in place. After a couple of snorting sounds, she brought her laughter under control. She squeezed Katy's arm. "I'm sorry. We shouldn't have laughed. But there you are in your little cap, looking so innocent, and then saying Jewel was *dissing* you." Trisha giggled again. "The word just doesn't fit you, Katy."

Katy sighed. "And being the attendant doesn't fit me, either." She thought about the lavender organdy waiting in Aunt Rebecca's shop. As much as she loved the shimmery fabric, she was foolish to think it would be enough to transform her into royalty. Tears pricked, irritating her with their presence. What was wrong with her lately? She always wanted to cry.

She squinted to hold back the tears. "Jewel said it would look stupid to have Michael standing up there alone. But how much more stupid will it look to have me standing there in my — as Jewel calls it — grandma dress and cap? No matter what I do, it'll be wrong!"

The buzzer rang, and students swarmed toward the doors. Katy, Trisha, and Cora joined the throng. Trisha got swept ahead, but Cora linked arms with Katy. She tipped her head and spoke directly into Katy's ear. "I have an idea. Make sure you meet me for lunch, and I'll tell you all about it." She scurried off to her locker.

Katy headed to her first-hour class. She had no clue what Cora would suggest, but she was open to anything that might solve her dilemma. For the first time in days, hope flickered in her heart. But when she sat down at the table at noon and heard Cora's idea, the hope sputtered and died.

"*That's* your idea?"

Cora's face sagged. She looked so defeated that Katy felt bad. Katy immediately apologized. Cora shrugged and sipped her milk, her eyes aimed off to the side. Her feelings were still hurt.

Trisha picked up a fish stick and waved it at Katy. "Actually, it's not a bad idea at all. I mean, think about it." She used the fish stick to trace tally marks in the air. "Number one, the sophomore class has to be represented and that representative has to be you; number two, your dad won't let you buy a dress and what you have will *not* do; number three, Cora, Shelby, and I each have at least one perfectly good dress hanging in the closet just begging to be worn again; number four, you're staying with Shelby homecoming weekend, so it'd be really simple for us to get the dresses to you; and five" — she made a triumphant slash with the fish stick, sending little crumbs through the air — "wearing one of our dresses, you'll look like any other high school girl on homecoming night."

"*And*," Cora added, setting aside her pout, "you'll be all dressed and ready for the dance."

A little shiver of excitement wiggled down Katy's spine when she thought about the dance. She scanned the lunchroom and spotted Bryce two tables over, sitting with his usual group of guy friends. He glanced up, caught her looking, and smiled. She smiled back then quickly looked away. Her heart fluttered in her chest. What would Bryce think if he saw her in a dress other than her typical Mennonite dresses? He seemed to like her, but he'd never told her she was pretty. Would he tell her so if she wore clothes like the other girls?

And since when is being pretty so important, Katy? She pushed the inner reprimand aside and said, "I'll have to think about it."

Trisha munched a fish stick, her brow puckered in thought. She went on as if Katy hadn't spoken. "Cora's dresses will probably fit you better since you're closer to the same size — both of you are really short."

"Hey!" Cora protested.

Trisha laughed. "But I still love ya, *shorty*." She laughed again at Cora's sour face and then said, "You'll need to wear high-heeled shoes no matter which dress you choose." She peeked under the table. "But you have really little feet. Mine won't fit you. What size do you wear, anyway?"

"Six and a half."

Cora paused in carrying a forkful of macaroni and cheese to her mouth. "Are you kidding me? I haven't worn shoes that small since I was in sixth grade!" She looked at Trisha. "Shoes might be a problem."

Katy looked from Trisha to Cora. "Why can't I wear my church shoes?"

"Are they high-heeled?" Cora asked.

"Not really. They're kind of like my tennis shoes, only black, and — "

The other two girls groaned. They chorused, "Grandma shoes!"

Several kids looked in their direction and snickered. Katy's ears heated.

"You really need something else," Cora insisted. "Strappy, with a spiky heel. Something sexy, to match the dress."

Sexy? Katy got an uncomfortable feeling in her stomach. "But—"

Trisha shrugged. "Don't sweat it. We'll work it out."

"Yeah, Katy." Cora grinned. "Just trust us—we'll get you all taken care of. You'll *be* the sophomore attendant, and we'll show Jewel you belong up there as homecoming royalty."

Katy hurried through the hallway toward Mr. Gorsky's room. She'd looked forward to forensics class all day. Their principal interrupted fifth period and announced that the forensics team had earned nine medals and took third place overall in the tournament at Minneapolis, but he hadn't named the individual winners. Katy hoped Bryce had won a medal. She wanted to be able to congratulate him. She whirled around the corner and nearly ran directly into Marlys, who was moving in the opposite direction.

Marlys scowled. "Sheesh, watch where you're going. Is that hat blocking your view, or what?" She zipped past Katy and disappeared around the corner.

Katy stared after Marlys, irritation and embarrassment making her wish she could yell an insult that would cut

Marlys as deeply as Marlys often cut her. But even if she
thought of something, Katy probably wouldn't say it. She
didn't have the nerve, and she'd been taught to treat others the way she wanted to be treated. She only wished
Marlys — and a few other girls — had been taught the same
lesson.

Stifling a sigh, she entered the forensics classroom. She
sank into her familiar seat and watched her classmates
goof off, the way they always did before the bell rang.
Sometimes they continued even after the bell rang. Bryce
was in the midst of several other students, talking and
laughing. He caught her eye and grinned, and she hoped
he might separate himself from the group and come talk to
her. But he didn't. So she unzipped her backpack, removed
her forensics folder, and sniffed to control the sting of
tears.

Mr. Gorsky strode into the room and clapped his hands
together. "Everybody, take a seat and quiet down."

"But this is a celebration day, Mr. G," one of the boys
called. "After our victory in Minneapolis, don't we get a
day off?"

Mr. Gorsky shook his head. "Nope. We'll take our day
off after the final tournament. Until then, we've got work
to do. So settle down, gang."

With good-natured mutters, the students slouched into
their desks. As soon as everyone was seated, Mr. Gorsky
addressed the class. "This is very short notice, but I received a call today from the forensics coach at Hill City.
They're hosting a tournament on the twenty-seventh and
need two more schools to participate, or they'll have to
cancel."

"But that's the Saturday after homecoming." The reminder came from one of the senior girls. "We've got the dance after the game. It'd be pretty hard to get up for a tournament after being out so late."

Mr. Gorsky nodded and held up one hand. "I know, Whitney. That's why I initially didn't sign up for it, but — "

Marlys bustled into the room, waving a piece of paper. She handed it to Mr. Gorsky then dropped into the seat next to Bryce. Katy tried not to stare when Marlys tipped sideways and whispered something into Bryce's ear, and Bryce smiled and nodded in response.

Mr. Gorsky glanced at the paper then set it on the desk behind him. He went on as if Marlys hadn't interrupted. "There might be some of you who aren't planning to go to the dance."

Every student looked in Katy's direction. Fire lit her ears. She looked at Bryce. He didn't say a word. She blurted, "I'm going. With Bryce."

Marlys's jaw dropped. Some girls snickered. A couple of the boys burst into loud, abrasive laughter. Bryce ducked his head. Katy wished he'd tell the others to knock it off, that there wasn't anything funny about him going with her. But instead he shrank like a turtle disappearing into its shell.

Embarrassed and hurt, she turned her attention to Mr. Gorsky, hoping everyone else would follow her lead.

"All right, all right." Mr. Gorsky frowned at the class. The merriment faded. He glanced around the room. "No one can go? Are you sure? It'll be a small tournament, maybe eight schools total competing. We stand a good chance of walking away with the first-place trophy, especially if everyone performs as well as you did this past Saturday."

Still, no one said anything.

Their teacher lifted his shoulders in a brief shrug. "Well, if everyone's going to the dance, then obviously we can't do it. So I'll call the coach and tell him not to expect us."

The same girl who'd first protested stood up and faced the other students. "Come on, guys — isn't there *anybody* who could go? You can bet Salina High West is sending some of their thespians." She grinned, her eyes twinkling mischievously. "Wouldn't it be fun to stomp them in the forensics meet after stomping them in the basketball game?"

Murmurs broke across the group. One of the boys raised his hand. "I'm going to the dance, but I can still get up early and catch the bus to Hill City in the morning, Mr. G." A few others said, "Me too" and "I'll go."

Mr. Gorsky snatched up a pen and the paper he'd discarded earlier. He grinned, his mustache twitching. "Now we're talking." He began scribbling on the paper. "Okay, so Brad, Marjorie, Connie, John, Roger, and Donna are all a go. Anybody else?"

"Me," a girl named Eileen said as she sighed. "I'm better at reciting poetry than dancing, anyway."

"I'll say," one of the boys teased, and she smacked him on the shoulder. Several students laughed.

Mr. Gorsky added her name to his list. He tapped the pen on the paper. "That makes seven competitors. We need three more to make it worth the trip."

"I'm *definitely* going to the dance — with Michael Evans," Marlys said, shooting Katy a *sorry, you lose* look, "but I don't mind getting up early. I can always sleep on the bus if I need to catch a few extra Z's." She looped arms with Bryce. "So count us in. Right, Bryce?"

Bryce didn't say anything, but he nodded.

If Bryce was going, Katy was going. She jammed her hand into the air.

A couple of students tittered, but she ignored them.

Mr. Gorsky smiled. "And that makes ten. So we can get our school on the list of attendees." He set the paper aside. "Even though we've got enough competitors to make a team, I'd be happy to take more than ten of you. I need to call the coach in the morning and give him the list of names and categories, so if you want to go, please let me know before class is over today. Now — " he rubbed his palms together — "let's get to work."

Chapter Ten

The week after Bryce invited Katy to go to homecoming, she puzzled over a peculiar change in his behavior. Before, nearly every day, he stopped by her lunch table or caught her in the hallway to chat. In their shared classes, he'd never been shy about taking the seat next to hers or asking to borrow a pencil. But now if they encountered each other in the hall, he offered a quick "hi" — or, even worse, an embarrassed glance — and hurried on. He chose a desk several seats away even if the one next to her was open. Not once, Tuesday through Friday, did he approach "her" table in the cafeteria. In fact, he seemed to make it a point to avoid her.

If he caught her by herself — at her locker or in the classroom — he spoke to her the same way he always had before. But as soon as another student came around, he turned aloof. And in a school with as many students as Salina High North, someone *always* came around and cut short their time of relaxed conversation. She'd considered Bryce a friend, but now he seemed a stranger. Katy couldn't understand what she had done to change him.

On Friday at lunch, she gathered her courage and mentioned her confusion to Cora, Trisha, and Jewel. "I thought he liked me, but now I'm not so sure. Do you think he's changed his mind about taking me to homecoming and doesn't know how to tell me?" Images of Marlys and Bryce sitting close and whispering together in forensics class flashed in Katy's memory. The remembrance stung.

"Boys are weird, Katy," Jewel said in a bored tone. "If you're gonna pursue 'em, you just have to get used to it." Then she looked up, her gaze following something behind Katy. A conniving smile curved her lips. "And speaking of pursuing . . . there goes my prize catch. See you all later." She pushed away from the table, leaving her half-empty tray behind.

Katy peeked over her shoulder and watched Jewel saunter in her hip-swaying way to a group of older boys wearing leather letter jackets. When Katy spotted Tony Adkins in the middle of the boys, she knew who Jewel meant by the "prize catch." Jewel slipped herself underneath Tony's arm and snuggled close. He laughed, curling his arm around her waist. He winked at his friends then angled Jewel toward the hallway. The pair disappeared. Katy observed the other boys nudging each other on the shoulder and snickering before they headed to the lunch line.

She turned back and found both Cora and Trisha staring after Jewel with disapproving looks on their faces. Cora shook her head. "She's gonna get herself in trouble."

Trisha shrugged. "That's her issue. Jewel does what Jewel does, and she doesn't care what anyone thinks."

Cora glanced around, as if making sure no one was listening, then quirked her finger to invite Trisha and Katy to lean close. "Remember how she said she was going to get Tony Adkins to ask her to the dance?" She paused, waggling her eyebrows. "I heard she promised him a keg of beer if he took her."

"Beer?" Katy squawked.

"Shhh!" Trisha hissed.

Katy lowered her voice to a whisper. "But where would she get beer?"

Cora shrugged and lifted the half-eaten hamburger from her tray. "I dunno. Maybe her mom's boyfriend? Jewel said he's bought it for her before."

Katy gawked at Cora, who began eating as if nothing was wrong. She turned to Trisha. "We have to tell Shelby."

Trisha released a little snort. "As if Shelby could do anything."

"She could tell her parents. Jewel lives with them — she has to obey their rules."

Trisha laughed. "Katy, you are so naïve. Just because Jewel lives with the Nusses doesn't mean she *has* to do what they say. I mean, really, how many kids do everything their parents tell them to do?"

Katy knew of several kids who followed their parents' directions. Before she could answer, Trisha went on.

"Kids usually find a way to do what they want whether their parents approve or not — and Jewel is a pro at breaking rules."

"Well," Katy insisted, "I still think we should tell Shelby."

"She wouldn't listen! She's so caught up with Jayden, she doesn't care about anything else." Trisha broke off a chunk of her hamburger bun and jammed it in her mouth.

She spoke around the lump of bread. "It wouldn't make any difference if you told, except to torque Jewel off royally. Just let it go."

"But—" Katy started to argue.

Cora interrupted. "Katy, I've been thinking about Bryce and why he might've stopped talking to you."

Katy forgot about Jewel. She leaned toward Cora. "Why?"

"Well, you know how guys are—sometimes they torment each other, and sometimes they egg each other on?"

Katy thought about the group of boys who'd seemed to approve of Tony heading off with Jewel. She nodded.

"I wonder," Cora mused, "if some of the guys have been bugging Bryce. You know, giving him a hard time for asking you to homecoming. So to keep from being teased even more, he's kind of, I don't know, keeping his distance?"

"Yeah," Trisha said. "He could be protecting himself. It's nothing against you."

"But it bothers me." Katy thought about how she'd always looked forward to seeing Bryce, knowing he would smile and talk to her. Now when she saw him, her stomach felt heavy with dread instead of pleasure because she couldn't be sure if he'd acknowledge or ignore her. She hated the roller coaster of emotions. "Why can't we just be friends and be at ease with each other?"

Cora laughed. "You've never had a boyfriend, have you?"

Katy shook her head.

"Well, the thing with boys is, it's all about appearances." Cora pushed her tray aside and tipped her head, her eyebrows high. "Y'see, Katy, a jock might flirt with lots of different girls to get something from them, like maybe help with homework or—" Her face blushed briefly.

"Something else, but he'll only seriously date the popular girls or the cheerleaders. But a skater will *never* go after a cheerleader, because he knows it's pointless — she wouldn't give him the time of day. So, instead, he goes after a skater girl. A skater girl will win his buddies' approval and keep him in right standing with the group."

Cora sent Trisha a thoughtful look. "Bryce is kinda between groups, isn't he? He hangs with the good kids, and he gets really good grades so he fits with the smart kids, but since he's on the soccer team he also hangs with some of the jocks." She grimaced. "Kinda hard to know where to put him."

Trisha tore her remaining hamburger into little pieces and dropped them on her tray while she spoke. "I bet it's the other soccer guys who are riding him about asking Katy. He doesn't want to be teased, so he tries not to let them see him talking to her."

"That makes sense to me," Cora said.

The two acted as though they'd forgotten Katy was there. Katy smacked her fork onto her tray. Cora and Trisha both jumped and looked at her. Katy said, "So if I go to homecoming with him, is he going to hide from me all night, or will he actually spend time with me? Because I don't see any point in going if he isn't going to talk to me or act like I'm there." She'd never thought Bryce would treat her like so many other kids at school did, looking past her as though she didn't exist. Now they knew she existed — they wouldn't be able to ignore her on homecoming night when she represented the class — but Bryce pretended not to notice her. Being ignored by Bryce hurt more, because she'd trusted him.

Trisha and Cora exchanged a quick look. Cora said, "It's kinda hard to know what'll happen, Katy. Like Jewel said, boys are weird. Who can figure them out?"

"Yeah, but"—Trisha grinned—"they're *sooo* worth it." Both Trisha and Cora laughed.

Katy pondered Trisha's statement as she settled in her desk for fifth hour. The up and down feelings of happiness and despair had nearly driven her crazy the past few days. Was it worth the emotional upheaval just to have a date? If going on a date made such a change in a friendship, she wasn't sure she wanted the date. She'd rather have things go back to the way they'd been, when Bryce treated her like she mattered.

A woman Katy had never seen before stepped to the front of the classroom. "Good afternoon, class." A nervous kind of smile twitched the corners of the woman's lips. "I'm Mrs. Barnes, and I'm substituting for Mr. Harrison. I understand he intended to begin a group research project with you today, and he prefers to explain it himself. So he's asked that you to use the hour as a study hall."

Cheers erupted. Mrs. Barnes waved her hands. It took several seconds to restore order. She said, "If you don't have homework to work on, please read a library book."

From the back of the room, someone hollered, "Can I go to the library?"

"Me too," another student called.

At least three others also requested permission to go to the library. The woman sighed. "Yes, anyone who needs a book, go ahead." A dozen kids darted out the door. "The rest of you, please work quietly." She sank into the teacher's chair, seemingly relieved to be finished with her duty.

Katy's Homecoming

Katy had a library book in her backpack — she always carried one with her in case she finished an assignment early. She opened her backpack to remove it, but the sight of a spiral notebook captured her attention. A longing to release frustration welled up inside her, and she knew what would help. She opened the notebook to a clean sheet and smoothed the page flat. Leaning over the fresh lined sheet of paper, she began to write.

When we are alone
the friendship you share with me
is so sweet,
and it seems the beautiful world
which we have created
will never end.
But listen!
The sound of many voices grows louder
as the crowd
approaches.
And you disappear
not to be seen until the crowd
disperses.
Are you ashamed
of me?
Your departure hurts so.
But the pain leaves
when you return
and the time is sweet
until the crowd
returns
again.

She reread the poem. She'd want to make some changes before she recorded it in her journal at home, but it held the confusion she'd intended to convey. As she gazed at the neatly written lines, anger began to billow in her chest. It was *wrong* for Bryce to treat her one way when no one was around and another way when people were looking.

A little voice in her head chided, *But you're allowing him to treat you both ways. You gratefully accept whatever crumbs he throws at you, and you don't protest when he ignores you. So you're at fault too.* Even though she didn't want to admit it, she knew the inner voice was right. Bryce would go right on paying attention to her in private and ignoring her in public unless she found the backbone to stand up for herself.

She drew in a deep breath, imagining the oxygen infusing her with courage. *I have to talk to him.* But how could she talk to him when he avoided her like she had body odor each time other people were around? And people were *always* around! She let out a huff of aggravation, tapping her pen on the notebook. If her family had a telephone, she could call him at home, but she wouldn't dare call him from the grocery store in Schellberg where anybody could hear her and repeat what she said. So what could she do? *Tap, tap, tap* went the pen, fast and furious.

"Miss?"

Katy looked up. The substitute teacher was frowning at her. "Please use your pen for something other than a drumstick. Perhaps as a writing instrument?"

"Yes, ma'am," Katy said. And an idea struck.

Clamping her fingers around the pen, she flipped to a clean page. Either Bryce liked her or he didn't — he couldn't have it both ways. He'd better decide which way it would be. She pressed the pen's tip to the paper and began to write.

Dear Bryce, . . .

Chapter Eleven

I wonder if Bryce found my note. The thought wandered through Katy's mind as she climbed into bed Friday night. She'd slipped it between the vent slats in his locker. Hopefully, he'd checked his locker before he went home. Her heart pounded as she thought about him finding the folded note, opening it, maybe reading it where others would peer over his shoulder. *I hope he waited until he was alone to read it!*

She pulled the covers to her chin and let out a huge breath. *Thank goodness there are two days of no school!* At least she had a couple of days before she had to face Bryce again. Then she scowled into the dark room. When had she ever been glad she didn't have school? She loved school. She loved learning. But the past several days of dealing with some of the girls' spiteful comments and snooty looks, as well as Bryce's odd friendly-one-minute, unfriendly-the-next-behavior, had made her yearn for time away.

And she still hadn't decided what to tell Dad about being the attendant and going to the dance.

Scrambling out from under the covers, she snapped on the lamp beside her bed then scampered on bare feet across the wood floor to her desk. She yanked out her journal and a pencil then dove back into bed where she could stay warm. Folding a piece of paper in half, she formed two columns. She labeled them *Why I Should Go* and *Why I Shouldn't Go.* She chewed the pencil eraser, thinking. Finally she began to write, bouncing back and forth between the columns as reasons occurred to her.

When she finished, column one, *Why I Should Go,* held four statements:

The sophomore class will be unrepresented if I don't.
The kids don't need another reason to think I'm weird.
It's an honor, and an honor should be accepted.
I really, really, really want to see what it's like to be normal!!

Under *Why I Shouldn't Go* she'd recorded:

The fellowship doesn't approve of fancy clothes or dancing.
Dad worries about me getting caught up in worldly activities.
Bryce has been acting strange, so the evening might not be very fun.
There's a forensics meet the next morning, and I won't be as rested.

With four reasons under each, they appeared evenly balanced. Katy groaned, pulling the covers over her head for a moment. But which side had reasons that carried more importance? She lowered the quilt and examined the lists. The reasons under *Why I Should Go* were all selfish — Katy-focused. With the exception of the comment about Bryce's behavior, the reasons under *Why I Shouldn't Go* all honored someone else — the church fellowship, her dad, and her forensics coach and team.

She placed the notebook on the table beside her bed, flopped against her pillows, and stared at the ceiling. *It means I shouldn't go, doesn't it, God?* But would it really hurt, just this once, to do what she wanted to do rather than what others would have her do? She rolled to her side and looked at the list again. The first reason under the *Why I Should Go* column seemed to leap from the page.

Dad said she could decide, so whatever she chose, he wouldn't hold it against her. But her classmates wouldn't be so forgiving. If she made Michael Evans stand up there all alone, she'd never be able to live it down. She *had* to go. Didn't she? She snapped off the lamp, burrowed under her covers, and closed her eyes. She didn't want to think anymore.

Katy stayed home Saturday rather than working for her aunt at the fabric store. With Dad and Mrs. Graber's wedding only five days away, Dad wanted Katy to give their house some special cleaning. Katy had wanted to go into town so she could tell Aunt Rebecca to send the organdy fabric back to the factory. If Cora or Trisha loaned her a dress, Katy wouldn't need to sew one for herself. She hoped she would remember to talk to her aunt at worship on Sunday.

During breakfast, Dad said, "With Rosemary moving in, we need to make room for her. So I'd like you to clean out all the closets upstairs and down, including the one in my bedroom. Then organize the dresser in my room so there are some empty drawers for her use. Then — " A funny look crept over his face. "About your sewing room."

Katy jammed her fork into the mound of scrambled eggs on her plate but didn't lift a bite. Since she was a little girl, she'd called the third bedroom upstairs her sewing room even though there was more than just her mother's sewing machine in there. It had become something of a combined sewing room, study, and playroom. She loved having that extra space. "What about it?"

"Rosemary would like to turn the room into a guest room so if her children come to visit, they have a place to stay."

Katy swallowed. "They couldn't stay in town if they came, maybe with Grampa and Gramma?"

Dad's brows pulled down. "Now, Katy, that wouldn't be fair to your grandparents. They aren't running a hotel. We'd be taking advantage of them."

Mrs. Graber's been staying with Grampa and Gramma for several months. No one has seemed to think she was taking advantage. She held the argument inside. "But what am I supposed to do with my stuff?"

"I suggest you sort through everything and decide what you really need and what you don't. The things you need can go in your bedroom, and the other things you can box up to give away. I brought several boxes from the grocery store when I was in last week — the boxes are in my room. Just help yourself." Dad picked up a piece of toast and took

a bite. "I'm sure there are items that aren't really necessary. Having the extra room has turned you into something of a packrat." He smiled at her, indicating he wasn't
finding fault.

Katy still felt insulted. Everything in that room held
significance for her, and she didn't want to give any of it
away. "If I want to keep everything, can I store the boxes
in the attic?"

Dad shook his head. "Sorry, Katy, there won't be room.
Rosemary has several pieces she wants to bring when she
moves in, so some of our things will go in the attic."

A sick feeling crept through Katy's stomach. She'd sus-
pected Mrs. Graber might make changes, but knowing it
would happen was harder than imagining it. "Like what?"

"Well, like the china cupboard and dishes. And the dining room table and chairs."

Those are things my mom used! Katy's throat felt too
tight to force out words.

Dad went on, "They're going to the attic because I don't
want to give them away. At least, not yet. You might want
them when you marry and move into your own house. If
you decide you'd rather not have them then — "

"I want them." Her voice sounded squeaky, but at least
she could talk. "And I'll want to take a lot of the things I
have in the sewing room too. So can't I put them in the
attic?" Tears stung, and she sniffed hard to prevent them
from escaping. "I'll push the boxes clear under the eaves
so they won't be in the way. Please?"

Dad sat quietly for a few seconds, but finally he nodded. "All right, if you can push them out of the way, then
I'll let you keep what you want to." He sighed. "I suppose

you're having to make enough adjustments without giving away your belongings."

Katy knew she should appreciate his consideration, but at the moment she was still a little mad at him. She'd try to be grateful later. "Sounds like I've got a lot to do today, so I better get started." She began clearing the table, even though Dad was still munching a piece of toast.

Dad leaned back, so she wouldn't bump him when she took his plate. "Rosemary will be out sometime this afternoon to finish your dress for the wedding. She said it just needs to be hemmed, so that shouldn't take very long. Maybe she'll have time to help you in the guest room."

It's my sewing room, not a guest room. "I can clear it out by myself." She didn't want Mrs. Graber going through her things, even if the woman was going to be her stepmother.

"It's a big task. Don't be afraid to ask for help if you need it," Dad said. "I'll be out in the barn, but if you need me, just holler." He popped the last bite of toast into his mouth and pushed away from the table. He caught Katy's shoulders with one arm and gave her an awkward hug. "I know things are changing, Katy-girl, but it will all be fine. You'll see."

It will all be fine. Dad's words echoed through Katy's mind as she worked. Clearing Dad's closet and dresser proved simple — Dad had never put things in the places left vacant when Katy's mom decided to leave, so all Katy had to do was organize his clothing. Mrs. Graber would have plenty of room to hang her dresses and put clothes in the dresser.

The sewing room proved more challenging. She wasted precious minutes examining items and conjuring memories of when she'd received them, who'd given them to her, or an especially enjoyable use of them. The small trunk where she'd placed items her mother left behind proved the most distracting. Katy had no idea how long she sat idle, fingering the embroidered handkerchiefs, the yellowed head covering with its trailing black ribbons, and a dried flower bouquet, which her mother had carried when she married Dad.

As Katy touched the things her mother had once held, a lump filled her throat, and she slammed the top of the trunk before the lump turned into tears. Katy decided she couldn't *think*, she'd just have to *pack*, and the cleanup went much faster. By noon she had boxed everything that was unnecessary with the contents labeled neatly on the box tops. Even though cold wind whistled through cracks around the windows, Katy was sweaty from exertion. She needed a break.

But I have to fix lunch for Dad and me. So much for a break. But in a few more days, Mrs. Graber would be Mrs. Lambright. Dad's wife. And Mrs. Lambright would fix Dad's lunch. Katy couldn't decide whether she was relieved or resentful about someone else taking over her long-held duties. Nothing seemed simple these days.

As she clumped down the stairs, a good smell reached her nose. She paused for a moment and sniffed, savoring the mixed aromas of meat, vegetables, and bread. Her nose made an identification: beef stew and biscuits. Had Dad been cooking? She skipped down the stairs and hurried into the kitchen. Mrs. Graber stood at the stove, stirring a big pot. Steam billowed around the stove, scenting the air. Katy watched her lift the spoon, blow on its contents, then take a hesitant sip. She smiled, nodded in satisfaction, and placed the lid on the pot. When she turned and spotted Katy, she jumped.

"Oh my, Kathleen! I didn't hear you come in. You nearly scared me out of a year's growth."

Katy swallowed a chuckle. The saying always sounded funny coming from an adult, since adults didn't grow any more. At least not in height. She coughed to cover another bubble of laughter she didn't want to have to explain. "I'm sorry. You surprised me too. I didn't know you were here."

"I came out early. Your dad told me he intended to have you clean out the spare bedroom today, and I knew it would be a big task. I thought you might appreciate someone else fixing lunch." Her face puckered in sympathy. "Are you as worn out as you look?"

Katy hadn't peeked in a mirror, so she had no idea how she looked, but she felt worn out. "I am tired," she admitted.

"Well, you sit down there and relax while I finish putting lunch on the table." Mrs. Graber bustled around removing bowls and silverware from cupboards and drawers, as at ease as if she'd lived in Katy's house for years. "Your dad will be in soon, and then we'll eat."

Katy sat, but she couldn't relax. It felt too strange, watching Mrs. Graber work and not helping. She was glad when Dad came in, and everyone sat down. Dad prayed, then Mrs. Graber dished stew for each of them. The stew was delicious with tender, well-seasoned chunks of beef, crisp-yet-tender vegetables, and a rich, onion-flavored broth thick enough to cling to a biscuit when Katy dipped one into the bowl.

Dad seemed to enjoy it too. He ate two bowlfuls and asked for a third. Mrs. Graber laughed. "I'm going to have to adjust my cooking to accommodate your appetite, Samuel. It's been several years since I cooked for more than one person." Tears suddenly appeared in her eyes, making the green irises even brighter. "But what a delight to be part of a family again."

Katy looked down at her bowl when Dad took Mrs. Graber's hand. She didn't know where this affectionate side of him had been hiding, and she didn't know whether she was happy or jealous. *Maybe I'll make two columns and try to figure out my feelings later on.* Not that the exercise had proved helpful before. Katy peeked through her eyelashes. Dad and Mrs. Graber were still sitting there, holding hands and looking at each other.

Katy cleared her throat. "Mrs. Graber?" The woman gave a little jerk. She looked at Katy. "May I have another biscuit? They're very good."

Mrs. Graber handed the biscuit plate across the table. "Of course, dear. They're good because I used your grand-mother's recipe." She turned her crinkling smile on Dad again. "I've always used buttermilk when I've made biscuits, but Ruth uses lard instead of butter. I didn't realize what a difference it could make."

Katy slathered butter on the biscuit and took a big bite. Before she'd finished chewing, Dad said, "Katy?" She gulped down the bite and looked at him. The serious expression on his face made her feel like the biscuit was caught in her throat. She took a quick sip of milk.

"Have you thought about what you want to call Rosemary after we're married?"

Katy blinked twice, her gaze flicking from Dad to Mrs. Graber and back. Would Dad expect her to call the woman *Mom* or *Mother*? "Um, no, I guess I haven't. She's just ..." Katy laughed self-consciously. "Well, she's been Mrs. Graber."

Mrs. Graber laughed softly too. "You're right. I've been Mrs. Graber for twenty-six years. Becoming Mrs. Lambright will be quite an adjustment."

Katy hadn't considered how many adjustments Mrs. Graber was making to marry Dad. But Mrs. Graber was leaving her town, her home, her family. She'd get a new name, a new church fellowship, a new stepdaughter. Maybe it was as hard for her to get used to as it was for Katy. The idea softened Katy a bit more toward the woman.

Mrs. Graber tipped her head, crunching one black ribbon against the shoulder of her dress. "I won't be Mrs. Graber anymore, and it would be silly for you to address me as Mrs. Lambright. Would you feel comfortable calling me Rosemary?"

Relief that no one suggested *Mom* flooded Katy. Her spine turned to Jell-O, and she slumped a little lower in her chair. Katy had never addressed an adult by his or her first name—Dad insisted she used the titles Miss, Missus, or Mister. But she supposed the rules were different for stepparents. She nodded. "Rosemary is ... is fine." Surprisingly, the name didn't stick on her tongue.

Mrs. Graber's face broke into a relieved smile. "Good. Rosemary it is. And, Kathleen, if you'd like to begin calling me Rosemary now, even though we haven't had the wedding yet, it's just fine."

Katy nodded, but she knew it would take some getting used to. She stood. "Would you like me to clear the table?"

Before either of the adults could answer, the crunch of tires on the hard ground intruded. Dad stepped to the window and looked out. He scowled. "It's a little yellow Beetle. Nobody around here drives a car like that."

Katy darted to Dad's side and peeked out. She grinned up at Dad. "I know who it is." She ran to the back door and swung it wide. "Shelby!"

Chapter Twelve

The doors of the Beetle opened and girls spilled out: Shelby, Cora, Trisha, and Jewel. Giggling, jostling one another, they ambled toward the house. Cora had a bulky duffel bag on her shoulder, and Trisha swung a plastic Wal-Mart sack. Shelby gave Katy a quick hug as she entered the kitchen, but the others just stepped in past her.

"What are you guys doing out here?" Katy latched the door and spun to face her friends. They'd never visited before.

Shelby laughed. "We would've called first, but since you don't have a phone ..." She shrugged, flashing a grin at Katy's dad, who stood beside the sink and looked from girl to girl with an uncertain expression. "I hope we aren't intruding."

"No. No, not at all," Dad said. "Katy's friends are always welcome." But he didn't sound sure of himself. He bobbed his hand in Mrs. Graber's direction. "Let me introduce you to my fiancée." Pink stained his cheeks. "This is Mrs. Rosemary Graber. On Thursday, she will become Mrs. Lambright."

Jewel hung back, quiet and watchful, but the others all smiled and offered friendly hellos to Mrs. Graber. Then Katy introduced each of the girls.

Mrs. Graber nodded. "It's very nice to meet you, Shelby, Trisha, Cora, and Jewel." She bestowed her bright smile on each of the girls in turn, getting every name correct. "Have you had lunch? There's stew and a few biscuits left. You're more than welcome to eat."

Shelby shook her head, the short blonde layers of her hair whisking around her face. "Thank you, but we went through the drive-through at McDonald's on our way out." She grinned broadly at Katy. "I wanted you to see my new car." Then she laughed. "Well, not *new*-new, it's a 2000 model. But it's new to me."

Dad looked out the window again. His brow puckered. "It's very ... bright."

Shelby laughed again. Katy hadn't realized how much she'd missed Shelby's cheerful presence until that moment. Having her friend visit made her want to laugh and cry all at the same time. Shelby crossed to Dad and peeked out the window too, as if to make certain the car was still there. "I really wanted a lime green Bug, but the dealership didn't have one. All they had was red or yellow. So I settled for yellow. I call it my little sunshine car. Colorful, but fun, right?" She grinned at Dad.

He nodded soberly. "Fun—and a very big responsibility."

Katy wished she could melt into the linoleum. How embarrassing to have Dad lecture Shelby. But Shelby just smiled and nodded.

"It sure is. And I promised my dad to be extra careful." She scurried to Katy's side. "If we're in the way, we can just show you the car and then go. But we hoped we might be able to visit for a little while ..."

Katy looked at Dad. He shrugged. "Take your friends upstairs, Katy. You know what chores you need to complete, but there should be time for a visit."

"Come on," Katy said before Dad could start listing the chores. She hurried toward the stairs, trusting the others to follow. When she reached her bedroom door, she paused on the landing and gestured everyone in. Shelby had been to Katy's house before, so she headed right in, but the others lagged, their eyes seeming to examine every inch of Katy's home. What did they think of the plain painted walls, scuffed wood floors, and pull chains hanging from bare overhead lightbulbs? For a moment, embarrassment spun Katy's stomach. But none of the girls said anything as they entered Katy's room and sat in a row near the foot of the bed.

Katy left the door open and crossed to her desk. She pulled out the chair and sat, facing the other girls. Cora, Trisha, and Jewel swiveled their heads, looking around, but Shelby looked at Katy. So Katy focused on Shelby. She didn't say anything, though. Never having had a group of friends from Salina visit, Katy wasn't sure what to do with them.

After sitting in silence for a minute or two, Shelby said, "I hope you don't mind us just dropping in. Dad said I could take the car for a drive, and we thought it would be fun come out."

Trisha added, "Besides, it gave us an excuse to bring our dresses and see if one of them might fit you. Homecoming's right around the corner, you know."

Katy knew.

Cora dropped the duffel bag between her feet and un-zipped it. She started pulling out dresses and tossing them across the bed. "I hope one of these will work."

Katy tried not to stare at the dresses. Glittering sequins, shiny satin, and sheer ruffles enticed her to hold one against her front and admire herself in the mirror.

Trisha held up the Wal-Mart sack. "We also brought some prom magazines to look at hair styles."

Katy zinged her attention to Trisha. "I can't get my hair done."

"Well," Trisha said, wrinkling her nose, "if you can't go to the hairdresser, then maybe Jewel can fix it for you." She bumped Jewel with her elbow, and Jewel grunted. "Jewel's pretty good at fixing hair. She can probably do any of these updos, and you wouldn't have to pay her."

"That's what *you* think," Jewel said, nudging Trisha in return. Then she shrugged. "But yeah, I like doing hair. So I'll fix it up for you, Katy, if you find a style you like."

The girls didn't understand. Katy couldn't be in pub-lic with her hair uncovered. She'd have to wear her cap. Before she could explain, though, Cora snatched up the emerald green dress and held it out to Katy. "This one's my favorite. Try it on."

Katy sucked in her lips and stared at the dress. Slender straps—no wider than a shoelace—led to a V-neck bod-ice covered in tiny sequins that caught the light. A wide satin band underlined the top, and a slim satin skirt with a sheer overlay fell from the band. Sequins formed a swirled design down one side of the overlay.

Katy fingered one of the skinny little straps. It was no wider than the ribbons that fell from her cap. How would she keep her bra straps hidden? She looked the dress up and down again, realizing the gown would provide less coverage than the full cotton slip she always wore under her clothes. Scandalous. Immodest. Guaranteed to shock Dad and the deacons. But she still wanted to try it on.

She hurried to the top of the stairs and called, "Dad?" She tilted her head and waited.

Mrs. Graber's voice replied. "He's out in the barn, Kathleen. Do you need something?"

"Nothing important," Katy called back. "I'll talk to him after my friends leave."

"All right."

Katy hurried to her bedroom and took the dress from Cora. "I'll go change in the bathroom."

"Oh, stay here, Katy, so we can see the transformation!" Cora begged.

Change in front of the girls? Katy's ears burned hot. "That's okay. You'll see after I put it on." She scurried out of the room before the others could argue. In the bathroom, she removed her dress, slip, bra, and shoes. Then she shimmied into the snug-fitting emerald dress. The little mirror above the sink didn't show much more than the bodice, which revealed expanses of Katy's chest never shown before. She crossed her palms over the bare flesh then slowly lowered them and made herself examine her reflection.

Creamy skin. Delicate collarbones. Narrow shoulders. She looked as good as the girls she'd glimpsed on the covers of fashion magazines in the aisle at Wal-Mart. She glanced down her length, noting the skirt front reached the tops of her knees but sloped downward to mid-calf in the back. She wished she could see the whole thing at once. If she angled the mirror on her dresser, she could get a full-body view.

Tiptoeing to the door, Katy peeked out. The landing was empty. She zipped across the hallway and slammed herself into her bedroom. The four girls, all engrossed in magazines, looked up. Their jaws dropped. Their eyes widened. Trisha whistled.

Cora broke into a huge grin and scampered to Katy's side. She tugged one strap a little higher on Katy's shoulder then turned Katy in a circle. "Wow, girlfriend, it fits like it was made for you. You look fantastic!"

Katy felt another blush building, but this time of pleasure.

Then Jewel snorted. "For Pete's sake, you look ridiculous. You gotta lose the cap." Trisha and Cora giggled.

Katy believed she'd lost enough already, considering how many clothing items lay on the bathroom floor.

Shelby bounced up. "I gotta say, though, even with the cap, you're a knockout, Katy." She waggled one eyebrow. "If you end up wearing this, Bryce's gonna drop dead when he sees you in it."

Katy moved to her dresser and adjusted the mirror at an angle. She stepped back until she got a view of the dress from neckline to hem. It fit snug against her ribs and hips, showcasing every inch of Katy's slender figure. She touched the wide satin band that hugged her rib cage, amazed at how different she looked in this dress. She'd never felt so beautiful. Or so exposed. She should change into her own dress.

She started to head for the bathroom, but Jewel stepped into her pathway. Her hands caught Katy's cap and pulled it loose. She tossed it onto the dresser. Before Katy could protest, Jewel removed the pins holding Katy's heavy coil, and Katy's hair spilled down her back. Katy scrambled to capture the strands.

Jewel put her hands on her hips and shook her head. "Who'd've thought Katy was hiding all that under her cap? Look at it." Jewel pushed Katy's hands aside and plunged her hands into Katy's thick hair. She gathered it in a loose poof. "What a head of hair!"

"And the color's so pretty," Cora said. "Brown with some gold — like chocolate and caramel swirled together." Cora touched her own straight dark brown hair. "I wish my hair was that color."

Katy ducked away from Jewel and picked up her cap. "I need to put this back on."

"I can't do your hair with that in the way," Jewel said, her tone sharp.

"But — "

"Oh, let her play with it, Katy." Cora put her clasped hands under her chin and gave Katy an imploring look. "I want to see what you look like with your hair done all pretty."

Trisha dug through the duffel bag. "We brought a curling iron and some jeweled bobby pins, so we could experiment." She held the items aloft. "See? All prepared."

A part of Katy longed to let Jewel, as Cora had said, play with her hair. But the longer they stayed up here, the more likely it became that Dad or Mrs. Graber would check on them. "I can't right now," she said, regret making her chest feel tight. "I have work to finish, and Dad'll be upset if I don't get it done."

Jewel rolled her eyes. "All right then. Spoil our fun."

Katy hesitated. Should she disappoint her friends or disappoint Dad? With a sigh, she said, "I'm sorry, but I really have to finish my work."

"That's okay, Katy, we did barge in on you." Shelby began folding the dresses scattered across the bed and stuffing them into the duffel. "Go get changed while we clean up in here."

Katy scurried off before anyone else voiced a protest. It took a little time to get her hair pinned up again. By the time she returned, the others had put everything away and even smoothed the coverlet on her bed. One magazine lay on her desk, open to a page showing three girls in fancy dresses. Katy pointed to the magazine. "You forgot one."

"No, I didn't," Trisha retorted, grinning. "I left it on purpose. See the girl in the middle?"

Katy leaned forward and peeked.

"I love the way her hair's done—the swoops on the side and all the curls pulled up in the back. Jewel said your hair is just the right length for that style. What do you think?"

Katy smoothed her finger over the glossy page, admiring the girl's hair. It did look nice. She also liked the dress, a pink, frothy-looking gown that went all the way to the floor and had a scrunchy, mesh-looking cape covering the girl's shoulders and upper arms. She pointed to the dress. "This is pretty too. Do you have a dress more like this one that I could borrow?"

Trisha made a face. "You can't wear something like that to homecoming. That's a prom dress."

Katy frowned. "What's the difference?"

Cora stepped forward and started flipping pages, pointing to dresses similar in style to the pink one. "These are
prom dresses, Katy. See how they're, like, huge and poofy
with all the frills and stuff? A homecoming dress is more, I
don't know, simple. Kind of like a cocktail dress."

Katy had no idea what Cora meant by a cocktail dress,
but she could see the difference between the dresses on
the page and the one she'd tried on. So she nodded.

Trisha said, "Look at the hairstyles and pick one you like."

"And I'll leave the dress you tried on so you can find a
hairstyle to match it," Cora added, grinning. "Besides, you
might want to model it for your Schellberg friends. I bet
they'll think it's to die for!"

Katy doubted she'd let Annika or anyone else see it.
But she might put the dress on and look at herself again
later — after Mrs. Graber went home and Dad was asleep.

The girls all moved toward the hallway with Shelby
leading the way. Katy followed. She wished they weren't
going, but she wouldn't get the sewing room done if she
didn't get back to work.

In the kitchen, Mrs. Graber sat at the table sorting
through a box of sewing notions. She paused and smiled at
the girls.

"Leaving already?"

They nodded, and Shelby said, "Yeah, we don't want to
keep Katy from finishing her chores. Thanks for letting us
stop by, though. It was nice to meet you. Congratulations
on your wedding and everything."

Cora, always the curious one, stepped close to Mrs.
Graber and touched the dress spread across the table top.
"Whatcha working on?"

Mrs. Graber's eyes twinkled. "Kathleen's dress for our wedding ceremony on Thursday. She's serving as my attendant."

Cora giggled. "She's getting to be the attendant all over the place, isn't she?"

Trisha bopped Cora on the arm. Cora yelped and glared at her. Rubbing her arm, she hissed, "Whaddid you do that for?"

Trisha just scowled.

Mrs. Graber's brows pulled down briefly, but then she smiled. "I'm so glad you girls came out and spent some time with Kathleen. As her father told you, you're welcome anytime."

"Thanks," they chorused, then Katy ushered them to the door. She walked them out to Shelby's car and said her good-byes there. After they drove away, she hurried back into the kitchen.

Mrs. Graber stood waiting, holding the nearly finished dress. "Would you try this on for me so I can pin the hem? I want to be certain the length is right."

"Sure," Katy said. She took the dress upstairs and quickly changed. As she turned to leave the room, she glimpsed her reflection in the mirror. She froze, giving herself a thorough examination. Mrs. Graber was an excellent seamstress—the pale orchid sateen dress fit Katy perfectly. So had the emerald green dress, but the effect was very different.

"Are you ready?"

Katy jumped at the sound of Mrs. Graber's voice outside the bedroom door. She trotted to the door and opened it. Mrs. Graber looked Katy up and down. Her face creased into a pleased smile. "It looks as if it fits. Does it feel all right on? I know the sateen is a stiffer fabric, so we don't want it too tight or you won't be comfortable." She began gently pulling at the caped shoulders, sleeves, and waist. Katy stood unmoving, allowing Mrs. Graber to check the fit.

Finally Mrs. Graber stepped back. "I don't think we'll need to do even a smidgen of altering. All that measuring beforehand paid off."

Katy smoothed her hands over her hips. The fabric felt cool beneath her palms. "It fits fine." Suddenly, a sparkle of green caught her attention, and heat filled her face. Cora had left the emerald dress hanging on Katy's closet door, and Katy had forgotten to put it away!

Mrs. Graber must have seen Katy's gaze shift, because she turned and looked at the dress too. Her eyebrows rose. "My, that's very pretty. Does it belong to one of your friends?"

Katy swallowed. "Yes. Cora. It's her homecoming dress." She hadn't lied — it was Cora's homecoming dress. Yet she felt deceitful anyway. She hurriedly pulled the dress down and opened her closet to hang it out of sight.

Mrs. Graber took the dress from Katy. She held it out, looking it over. Her face remained expressionless, but Katy bit down on her lower lip, wondering what Mrs. Graber was thinking. Finally Mrs. Graber gave it back. "It's quite exquisite with all the sequins and real satin. A very elegant dress."

Katy held the dress to her thumping heart, looking into Mrs. Graber's face. She hadn't acted shocked or dismayed. So Katy braved a question. "What do you think it would look like ... on me?"

Mrs. Graber didn't even hesitate. "I think a dress like that would look lovely on anyone. It's very flattering. The real question is, if you wore it, would it be a true reflection of the wearer?"

Katy blinked twice, confused.

"It's a very lovely, very worldly dress, Kathleen. And you're a very lovely Mennonite girl. It would be up to you to determine whether the dress is 'you' or not." A tender smile lifted the corners of Mrs. Graber's lips. "In my experience, one can't be content unless she's living in the way God intends her to live. Now — " Her hand stretched out and grazed Katy's arm, a motherly touch. "Come downstairs so I can get the hem for your attendant dress pinned, hmm?" With another soft smile, she turned and left Katy's room.

Chapter Thirteen

Monday when Katy got off the bus, her knees quivered.
All weekend she'd worried about what Bryce would say or
do after reading her note. Oh, if only the fellowship would
approve the use of telephones! Then she could have called
him and eliminated all this worry. But fussing about the
lack of phones wouldn't solve anything.

Cold, damp wind pressed her back, and she scurried
across the yard to her usual waiting spot near the front
doors. Because the bus dropped her off early, only a few
other students mingled in the yard. She wished Trisha,
Cora, or Shelby would hurry and arrive so she didn't have
to wait alone. Shelby would probably drive herself and
Jewel to school today since she had a car. Katy crinkled
her brow, fighting a small wave of jealousy. She was old
enough to get her license and drive, but Dad probably
wouldn't buy her a car. If she continued at Salina North,
she'd be riding the bus until she graduated.

She hugged herself, shivering, and watched cars turn
into the parking lot. When she spotted Shelby's little
yellow Beetle, Katy heaved a sigh of relief. She'd have

company soon. But instead of coming to the doors, Shelby trotted across the yard to join Jayden and his friends, and Jewel made a dash for the group of seniors where Tony Adkins was the center of attention. When Bryce got to school, would he come stand with her, or would he find another group to join? She didn't want to consider that he might continue to avoid her, so she pushed the thought away.

Soon Cora and Trisha arrived; Cora's mother dropped them off at the curb. They scurried directly to Katy and huddled close.

"Brr!" Cora shuddered. "It's so cold this morning. Saturday and Sunday were nice, but now it's cold again."

Trisha hunched her shoulders, bringing the furry collar of her jacket around her ears. "Good ol' Kansas — it never can make up its mind when it comes to weather."

Cora nudged Trisha and bobbed her head in Jewel's direction. "She's still cozying up to him. Think he'll really ask her to the dance?"

"Nah." A little cloud puffed around Trisha's face. "He's just using her. But she's too dumb to see it."

"Yeah." Cora sounded sad. "You know, she irritates me sometimes." She snorted. "Actually, she irritates me a *lot*, but I feel kind of sorry for her. She wants to be popular so bad, she'll do almost anything."

"Pathetic, isn't it?" Trisha shook her head.

Katy listened to the other two girls without contributing, her heart thudding. Even though she knew they were talking about Jewel, they could have been talking about Katy. She wanted to be accepted in the school too.

Cora grimaced. "I just hope she doesn't get so wrapped up with Tony that she ends up, you know, in real trouble."

Trisha nodded. "Me too. 'Cause if something bad happens, he'll make sure she gets the whole blame."

Cora crinkled her forehead. "You know what I can't figure out? She's living with the Nusses. Shelby's dad is a preacher, so you know Jewel's getting taught right from wrong. Wouldn't you think she'd start to, I don't know, change her ways?"

The buzzer blared, inviting the students to enter the building. Trisha hollered over the sound as the girls turned toward the door, "Yeah, but Jewel spent most of her life with her mom, who didn't do a very good job of teaching her to make good choices. What you grow up with, that's usually what you become."

Katy got separated from Cora and Trisha in the crowded hallway, but during her first-hour class, Katy couldn't stop thinking about what they'd said about Jewel. And she couldn't set aside the thought that their words applied to her in some ways. Did she really want to be like Jewel? She also couldn't stop worrying about second hour when she'd see Bryce. If he'd read her note, he'd know she expected him to either treat her like a friend — or not.

Please let him decide to be friends. The plea turned into a prayer. She missed his friendliness as much as she missed time with Shelby. It didn't seem fair that she'd have to lose both of them all at once.

Katy entered the algebra classroom and headed for her familiar desk — second row, the seat closest to the door. But then she moved past the first desk and sat in the next one. Her heart pounded so hard she could hear the thud in her ears. She'd left the desk empty for Bryce, but would he take it? Other students entered the room, talking and laughing.

But she didn't turn around to watch for Bryce. She faced forward, her hands linked on the desk, her breath coming in little spurts of nervous anticipation. Would he sit by her?

The desks on Katy's right filled. The one on her left remained open. Then shoes scuffed on the floor. The desk squeaked as someone sat down. Katy squeezed her eyes closed for a moment, her mouth dry. *Please, please let it be Bryce!* Then she peeked sideways. A girl named Liz sat in the seat. The buzzer rang, which meant class would begin. Katy whirled around and searched the room. Bryce sat in the next to the back row, on the opposite side of the classroom. His book was out already, so he'd been there long enough to get settled.

She jerked to face the front. Tears stung. She'd given him an ultimatum, and he'd made his choice. She just wished it didn't have to hurt so much.

Somehow Katy made it through the day. In her other classes with Bryce, she kept her head down and didn't try to make eye contact with him. She didn't hear much of the teachers' instructions; she was focused on not crying. Why had she given him that note? If she could take it back, she would. At least then she might get to talk to him now and then. Not talking to him at all—not being acknowledged by him at all—was awful.

Last hour—forensics—arrived. Forensics was so different from the other classes. No sitting in desks for lectures. The students mingled in groups, performing for each other. How would she be able to avoid seeing Bryce? She didn't think she'd be able to enter the classroom. But she had to. She'd signed up for the Saturday meet. Mr. Gorsky was counting on her. She couldn't skip the class.

Hugging her backpack, she lowered her gaze and scuttled into the room. She shot straight to the corner and sat, cradling her backpack in her lap like a shield. Then she stared at the door, watching the other students enter. When Bryce came in, Marlys was hanging on his arm the way she always did in forensics. Before Katy could witness him ignoring her, she shifted sideways in the seat and pretended to look for something in her backpack.

Mr. Gorsky moved to the front of the classroom and began sharing the assignments for the week, like he did every Monday. Katy heard her teacher's voice, but she didn't really listen to the words. So when he said, "And let's start with Kathleen," she had no idea what she was supposed to do.

She stared at her teacher, unblinking.

Mr. Gorsky stared back, his head tipped to the side with a slight smile underlining his mustache. He said, "Come on. We need to get going."

Katy gulped. "Going? Where?"

Someone snickered. Katy didn't even need to look to know it was Marlys. Katy's ears burned.

Mr. Gorsky cleared his throat. "Not *where*, Kathleen — what." He sounded very patient, not at all annoyed, but Katy still wanted to hide. She felt every eye in the room boring into her. "Come up and give your speech for us so we can offer critiques."

Katy's gaze slipped sideways and collided with Bryce's. As soon as their eyes met, he jerked his head and looked away. Katy's throat began to ache with the desire to cry. She wouldn't be able to speak with her throat all tight. She felt like someone had tied her tonsils in a knot. "N-now?"

She swallowed, trying to rid her voice of the squeakiness. "But it's Monday." Usually they performed for one another on Thursday.

Marlys snorted. "Didn't he just say this week's all messed up because of homecoming? So we're practicing today. Sheesh!" A few snickers followed her comment.

Embarrassment flooded Katy's face with heat. She ducked her head, battling tears. "I, I ..." She didn't know what to say.

Mr. Gorsky crossed over to her desk and spoke softly. "Kathleen, are you sick?"

Sick at heart. She managed a miserable nod.

He pointed to the door. "Take a break. Get a drink. If that doesn't help, go to the office and tell the nurse you're not feeling well."

Katy rose, her legs shaky. She wanted to thank her teacher, but her voice wouldn't work. So she just walked out the door with stiff steps. Outside the room, she collapsed against the brick wall. The cool brick felt good on her hot back. A voice rumbled from the other side of the door, and the room broke into laughter. Were they laughing at her?

She didn't want to know. She bolted from the wall and scurried toward the office. She'd convince the nurse she needed to lie down for a while. And while she was lying on the cot in the nurse's little station, shut away from everyone, she'd figure out how to avoid being around Bryce for the rest of the year.

Chapter Fourteen

Katy scuffed down the hallway that led to the nurse's station behind the school office. She kept her head down, blinking back tears. Her chest ached with the effort of holding her hurt inside. Someone called her name, but she didn't slow her steps. She wanted to get to the nurse's station and hide from the world. But then footsteps clattered up behind her and a hand grabbed her elbow.

"Hey, girl, what's your rush? Didn't you hear me?"

Katy looked into Jewel's grumpy face. She pulled her arm loose. "I'm going to the office." Students weren't supposed to loiter in the hallway during classes — the school handbook said so.

"Did the teacher alert the office that you're on your way?"

Katy shook her head.

"Then no one will know if you stop for a minute," Jewel said.

Jewel knew so many ways to get around the rules. But that didn't mean Katy should break them too. "But —"

Jewel put her hand on her hip and cocked her head. "Look, I know something you need to know, and I think

it's better for you to hear it when no one else is around."
She gestured to the empty hallway. "See how we're alone?
Perfect. So listen up."

Katy sighed. "Hurry then."

"You know how I've kept saying there's gotta be something wrong, the seniors choosing you as sophomore rep?
Well, they're playing a secret prank, and they've made you
part of it."

Katy frowned. "What do you mean?"

Jewel grinned, seeming to enjoy divulging the secret.
"The joke is really on Michael Evans. The senior boys
on the basketball team don't like him because he's just a
sophomore but he gets to start. And he showboats. That
really ticks them off. So they convinced the others to vote
you in as the sophomore girl attendant with him as the
boy. They figured you wouldn't do it — or if you did, you'd
show up in your granny dress and cap — so he'd end up
either standing out there alone or with 'the little Amish
girl,' as they call you. They want him to look like a fool."

Katy said the only thing she could think of. "I'm not
Amish."

Jewel rolled her eyes. "I *know* that. The point is, you
were chosen to make Michael look like an idiot. So ..." She
glanced up and down the hallway. "What are you gonna
do?"

Katy's knees felt weak. A joke? They were using her to
play a joke? She had no idea what to say or do. So instead
of answering, she turned around and went to the nurse's
station. The nurse accepted her statement that she wasn't
feeling well — the tears swimming in Katy's eyes were
probably convincing — and allowed her to lie down on the

cot until the closing bell rang. At the end of the school day, Katy retrieved her books and coat from her locker and hurried out to the bus without talking to anyone. The other students' laughter and noisy conversations made her want to yell at them to stop being so happy. *How dare they be so happy when she was so miserable?*

Katy slumped into the bus seat and pressed her forehead against the cold window pane. She couldn't wait to get home, go up to her room, and pour her thoughts and feelings into her journal. She felt like she might explode, so many emotions swirled through her middle. How could Bryce say he liked her then treat her like she didn't exist? How could she be the attendant now, knowing she was only chosen to play a joke on someone?

I'm a joke to them — just a joke. I don't fit in and they all know it. Bryce must know it too. That's why he doesn't want to take me to homecoming anymore. Why be seen with the school joke?

The bus rolled to a stop at Katy's corner, and Katy plodded to Dad's truck. She didn't try to smile or talk as she climbed in. She didn't care if Dad noticed she wasn't her usual self. Maybe he'd ask her what was wrong. She wanted him to ask, even though she probably wouldn't tell him. But if he asked, she'd know he cared.

But Dad just sent a quick smile across the cab and turned the truck toward home. His fingers drummed on the windowsill, the way they did when he was impatient about something. *Great, having to pick me up is keeping him from something else that's more important.* Katy clamped her jaw so tight her teeth ached, but it kept her from bursting into tears.

When Dad pulled into the yard, he finally spoke. "Katy, can you help Caleb with the milking tonight? Rosemary and I need to go to the church and talk to Deacon Pauls about our wedding service, and I've got to clean up before I go. I won't have time if I do the milking."

So Katy wouldn't be able to run up to her room and write. She clamped her jaw even tighter and managed a quick nod.

Dad frowned. "Katy-girl, what's wrong with you?"

If he'd sounded sympathetic instead of irritated, she might have spewed her frustration just to be rid of it. But his tone didn't invite her to share her thoughts. She snapped, "Nothing."

Dad's frown deepened. Katy hopped out of the truck and hurried inside the house before he said anything else. In her room, she threw her backpack into the corner and yanked a work dress from the closet. Minutes later, she stomped down the stairs and charged toward the kitchen, but she stopped when she heard Dad's voice.

" — surly mood today. I think she's sulking about the wedding."

Another voice answered. "Well, Samuel, our marriage will bring so many changes for Kathleen." Katy recognized Mrs. Graber's voice. And the woman's tone held the sympathy Katy had needed from her dad. "She's bound to be a little upset and worried. We just need to be patient with her while she adjusts."

Even though Mrs. Graber and Dad were wrong about Katy's reason to be upset, Katy was glad to hear Mrs. Graber ask Dad to be patient. She tipped her head, listening for Dad's reply.

"Confused and worried or not, I won't tolerate a sullen attitude. It's disrespectful. We shouldn't have to be subjected to that."

Katy's shoulders slumped. Why couldn't Dad try to understand? Her fingers itched to write, write, write. But she had to milk the cows. She set her feet down hard and made lots of noise as she moved through the house toward the kitchen so they would know she was there. When she entered the kitchen, Dad sent her a warning look, but Mrs. Graber smiled warmly.

"Thank you for filling in for your dad tonight," Mrs. Graber said. "I brought a casserole, so you won't need to fix supper too. Will that give you enough time for your homework?"

The woman's consideration warmed Katy, but for some reason Katy felt a prickle of resentment at the same time. Why should someone not related to her, someone who wasn't even a friend to her, be so considerate when the people who were supposed to care the most about her—like Dad and her closest friends, Shelby and Bryce—were ignoring her? She swallowed the sadness that filled her throat.

"It's fine. I don't mind helping. And yeah, I'll get my homework done with no problem."

Dad's forehead pinched. "Katy, you know I don't care for slang."

Katy blinked, trying to think of what she'd said. Then she realized she'd said "yeah" instead of "yes." She nearly rolled her eyes. Why did Dad have to be so picky? He'd have reason to complain if she brought home some of the other words she'd heard at school. Most of them were a lot worse than "yeah."

"You might also," Dad continued, "thank Rosemary for providing supper for us."

That'll be her full-time job in another few days, Katy's thoughts sniped, *so why should I say thanks?* She was taking her irritation with the kids at school out on Dad. She recognized it, but at that moment she didn't care enough to correct it. She needed a target, and Dad was available.

"I better get out to the barn. Caleb'll be here soon." She brushed past Dad, ignoring his stormy look. As she slammed out the door, she heard Mrs. Graber's gentle voice: "Give her time, Samuel. She's — "

Katy didn't hang around to hear what else Mrs. Graber would say in her defense. When she was halfway across the yard, Caleb's sedan pulled in. She hurried into the barn rather than wait for Caleb. Katy pulled a pair of Dad's coveralls over her dress. The zipper proved stubborn, and Caleb strode in and caught her wrestling with it.

He frowned, his freckles crunching together on his forehead. "You're milking tonight?"

"Yes." She gave the zipper pull a yank, and it whizzed to her chin. She shot Caleb a challenging look. "Is that a problem?"

He shrugged. "Figure it means I'll be doing most of the work."

We'll just see about that. "Go honk the horn so the cows know it's time," she said then whirled and stomped into the milking room.

The cows lined up, just as they always did, outside the double doors that led to the milking room. They filed in four at a time and stood complacently beside the milking machines. Katy knew the routine so well she could attach the suction cups and flip the switches in her sleep. But she stayed focused, determined to keep up, cow for cow, with Caleb. Although the February temperature was cold, she worked up a sweat and loosened the zipper on the coveralls midway through milking.

The rumble of the machines made conversation impossible unless they hollered, so she and Caleb worked without speaking. She noticed him glancing across the machines now and then, though, and she thought she saw surprise in his eyes. Although she didn't really enjoy milking, it gave her satisfaction to disprove his comment about having to carry the workload.

The last cows ambled out, and the milking room seemed deathly quiet with the machines off. Caleb stretched his arms over his head, lifting his chin and rotating his head side to side as if he needed to work out lots of kinks. Katy wanted to do the same thing, but she didn't. Why should she let Caleb know her back and shoulders ached from the fast pace of the past two hours?

When Caleb finished stretching, he grinned. "You wanna wash down the walls, or do you want me to?"

"Dad usually has you do it, so go ahead," she retorted, heading for the door to the tank room so she could check the dials and make sure the temperature was adjusted correctly. She didn't really want to talk to Caleb. After their last conversation, when he'd gotten so angry, she hadn't even said hello to him when their paths had crossed.

She examined the dials on the big gray tank that always reminded her of an overgrown hippopotamus. Everything looked fine. The sound of water splashing against concrete walls roared, letting her know Caleb was cleaning. He

knew how to do his job—he didn't need her supervision—
so she strode outside. Mrs. Graber's car still sat in the
yard, but Dad's pickup was gone. For a moment, loneliness
struck. She supposed Dad and Mrs. Graber would go off
alone together a lot after they were married. She'd better
get used to being left behind.

She scuffed up dust with the toes of her tennis shoes
as she crossed to the cows' enclosure and wriggled the
latch on the gate just to be sure it was secure. The last
thing Dad wanted was one of their cows wandering down
the road. She climbed on the bottom rail of the fence and
peeked into the feeding boxes. To her relief, Dad had filled
the feeders with hay before he left. At least she didn't need
to get all dusty feeding the cows.

Her tasks complete, she returned to the barn to strip off
the coveralls and put them on the hook. As she hung them
up, Caleb sauntered out of the milking room. He sent her a
smirky grin.

"Well, Katydid, I gotta say, you surprised me. Figured
by now you'd forgotten how to milk."

*As if I could forget something I've done for as long as I
can remember.* She chose not to reply. Especially since he'd
called her Katydid, a nickname he knew she hated.

He went on, "I told the guys just 'cause you go to public
school, you haven't forgotten how to be a Mennonite girl.
You sure proved it today."

Katy swung around and stared at Caleb. "Why were
you and the guys talking about me?"

Caleb pulled back slightly, his brow puckering. "Guys
talk. You know that."

"But not about *me*. I don't like it."

He chuckled and shrugged the coveralls off of his shoulders. "Sorry, not much I can do about that. Guys are gonna talk no matter if you like it or not." Then he scowled. "But I stood up for you. Doesn't that count for anything?"

Katy nibbled the inside of her lower lip. It did count. And it bugged her that it counted. Why did it have to be Caleb defending her? Begrudgingly, she nodded. "I suppose. Thanks."

His grin returned. "No problem. I know we, uh, kinda had a fight the last time we talked." Red filled his freckled face. "I got madder than I prob'ly should've. Didn't like it much that you wouldn't go to the singing with me."

That was obvious.

"Still, my mom says I should appreciate your honesty. So ..." His voice trailed off.

Katy waited to see if he would apologize for his awful behavior that day, but he didn't. She didn't say anything either. She didn't have anything to say. She'd kept herself quiet a lot instead of talking today. A hysterical giggle built in her throat at the thought. She coughed a little bit to hold it at bay.

Caleb sighed. "Well, the milking's done. Guess I should go on home." He looked at her expectantly.

What was he waiting for? She said, "See you later then."

Caleb nodded, his face sad. He moved toward the barn doors, his head low and his hands pushed into his trouser pockets. Just before he reached the doors, Katy experienced the sudden urge to call him back to ask if he wanted to stay to eat some supper with her. *I must be really lonely if I want to spend time with Caleb Penner!* She pinched her lips tightly and held the invitation inside.

Chapter Fifteen

Katy went into the house, washed up at the kitchen sink, then lifted the tin foil on the casserole dish resting on the corner of the counter. Chunks of chicken, peas, carrots, and rice swam in a creamy sauce. The casserole smelled wonderful, and Katy's stomach growled. Then she looked at the empty table, and her hunger fled. She didn't want to sit there alone and eat. She'd wait for Dad and Mrs. Graber.

She glanced out the window. Dusk had fallen, and the sky looked pale gray. Gloomy. It matched her mood. The hour felt even later than six thirty. When would they return? She had no way of knowing how long they would visit with Deacon Pauls, but it would be best to have the casserole hot and ready when they returned. She turned the oven dial to 300 degrees — high enough to warm the casserole but not so hot it would scorch — and slipped the dish inside. Then she went upstairs to change out of her dress. Even though she'd put on coveralls, her clothes still smelled like the barn.

Her school dress lay at the foot of her bed, and she quickly swapped dresses. Her nose wrinkling in distaste, she scooped up the work dress from the floor and scurried to the closet. When she opened her closet to drop the dirty dress in her clothes basket, she glimpsed the green dress Cora had left for her. She paused, skimming her fingers along the sleek waistband then down the skirt. *Such a beautiful dress.* Right beside it, on a wooden hanger, hung the dress Mrs. Graber had sewn for Katy to wear in the wedding. Katy pulled both dresses from the closet and held them side by side.

The sateen fabric of the orchid wedding dress gave off a slight shimmer; the sequins on the emerald green dress flashed little dots of light. The caped bodice of the orchid dress ensured Katy would be modestly attired; the V-neck on the green dress ensured people would see more of Katy's throat and chest than she'd ever exposed before. The skirt of the orchid dress fell to Katy's mid-calf; the green one reached that length in the back, but the higher front meant Katy's knees would show.

The seniors picked me so I could embarrass Michael. The thought stung as much now as it had when Jewel told her about the prank. Katy put the orchid wedding dress back on the clothes rod and carried the green dress to her mirror. She held it to her front. *But the joke would be on them if I showed up in Cora's emerald dress with my hair all done pretty and makeup on my face. And Bryce would be so surprised.* A smile slowly climbed her cheeks.

"Katy-girl?" Dad's voice called from the bottom of the stairs.

Katy tossed the dress aside and dashed to the landing. "Yes, Dad?"

"Come on down and set the table," he said. "It's late."

With a sigh, Katy tromped down the stairs. Couldn't he at least thank her for taking over the milking before he started giving out orders? To her surprise, Mrs. Graber was nowhere in sight. "Where'd Mrs. — Rosemary go?"

Dad rummaged in the refrigerator, pulling out butter, bottled dressing, and a bowl of lettuce salad. "She went back to town."

Katy retrieved hot pads from the drawer and opened the oven door. A wonderful aroma met her nose. "She didn't want to eat with us?"

"She's eating with several of the ladies in town. They're showering her with gifts this evening."

Katy spun and gawked at Dad. "She's having her wedding shower *tonight*?"

"Yes." Dad plopped the items on the table and looked at her. "What's the matter?"

"I thought I'd be invited. I'm her attendant after all." Katy's voice came out louder and more angry than she'd intended.

Dad propped his hand on his hip and gave Katy a look that told her she'd better get herself under control. "With it being a school night, I told the ladies not to invite you. I knew you'd have homework, and if you went to the shower, you wouldn't have time to finish it."

I would've had time if I hadn't had to milk the cows. She was proud of herself for holding the argument inside.

"I thought it was best to have you stay home." Dad softened his tone. "I'm sorry if you're disappointed. I didn't realize it meant that much to you."

Katy blinked. She hadn't realized it meant so much either, until she'd been left out. She thought about the ladies all together, talking and laughing without her. Somehow the image got jumbled up with the senior class, talking and laughing about how they could use her to make Michael Evans look stupid. She had to blink more.

Dad put his hand on Katy's shoulder. "I'm very sorry, Katy-girl. I should have talked to you about it and let you decide whether to go or not."

Katy sniffed hard. She shrugged his hand away and reached into the oven for the casserole. "It doesn't matter." But it did matter. She dished up the casserole without speaking again, but her thoughts raged. *I might've gotten left out of the wedding shower, but I'm not going to get left out of being the attendant at school. They think they're playing a prank on Michael. But just wait — the real prank is going to be played by* me *on* them.

Tuesday morning Katy watched for Shelby's yellow Volkswagen. As soon as it pulled into the school parking lot, she trotted across the pavement and met Jewel as the girls stepped out of the car. "I need to talk to you."

Jewel tossed her long hair out of her face. "And good morning to you too."

Katy decided to ignore Jewel's sarcasm.

"Hey, Katy, see you in class." Shelby called over the top of the car. She lifted the handle on her rolling backpack and headed for the school. "'Bye, Jewel. Talk to you later."

"Yeah, right," Jewel muttered. "As if we ever see her these days." Then she offered a halfhearted grin. "'Course, with her hangin' with Jayden all the time, she isn't checking up on me then running to her folks to rat me out.

It works pretty well, to tell ya the truth. Now — " Jewel headed for the school too. She didn't have a backpack today. "Whaddid you want?"

Katy balanced her backpack on her spine and jogged alongside Jewel. "Are you still willing to do my hair for homecoming?"

Jewel came to a halt. She spun and stared at Katy. "You're gonna do the whole dress-up thing?"

Katy nodded. "Yes. But I need you to help with my hair. I only know how to do a bun." She gritted her teeth. A bun was for grandmas. *Nobody would be calling her a granny at homecoming!*

An inappropriate exclamation flew from Jewel's lips. She threw her head back and laughed. "This'll be so sweet — wait'll I tell Tony!"

Katy grabbed Jewel's arm. "No! You can't tell!"

Jewel glowered at Katy. "Why not?"

"Because ..." Katy scrambled for a reason. She couldn't tell Jewel she was trying to get even with the seniors. "I want it to be a surprise. Wouldn't that be better?"

Jewel's eyes gleamed. "Well, well, well, who would've thought little Miss Goody-Goody could be so conniving?" She laughed again. "Careful, girlfriend, I think I might be rubbing off on you." The buzzer blared, and both girls hurried toward the school.

Katy said, "You won't tell, right?"

Jewel flashed a grin. "Oh, don't worry. You can trust me." She dashed ahead.

Katy watched Jewel disappear into the crowd. She hoped Jewel would keep her secret. Katy slid onto her biology stool next to Shelby and opened her book. She heard a sniff, and she looked at Shelby. Shelby's eyes were red, and her chin quivered. Katy touched Shelby's arm and whispered, "What's wrong?"

Shelby shook her head, gesturing to the front of the room where their teacher stepped up to begin his lecture. Katy had a hard time concentrating, knowing Shelby was upset about something. When class was over, she stayed close to Shelby as they moved through the hall to their next class. She asked again, "What's wrong?"

Tears welled in Shelby's eyes. Katy had never seen her friend so distraught. Shelby whispered, "Jayden ... He—" She gulped twice. "He broke up with me this morning."

Katy's jaw dropped. "He did? But why?"

Shelby swished the tears away with her fingertips. "He said he isn't ready to date one girl exclusively. But that's just an excuse."

"How do you know?"

Pink streaked Shelby's face. "Because last night he came over and we were watching a movie ... He came on to me—you know, kissing and stuff. And I said I didn't want to." The girls reached the history classroom, but they paused outside the door. Shelby drew in a deep breath. "I know I shouldn't be sad about breaking up with someone who only wanted to see what he could get from me. I mean, honestly, why should I bend my morals to do something I really don't want to do just to please some guy? Girls who do that only end up regretting it. But I really liked Jayden. It hurts that I wasn't worth more than that to him."

Katy had no idea what to say to comfort Shelby. So Katy gave her friend's arm a squeeze that she hoped would communicate her sympathy.

Shelby offered a wobbly smile. "Oh, I'll be all right." She sighed. "I guess this means I'm not going to the homecoming dance, though." Shelby headed through the classroom doorway. Katy followed. Shelby said over her shoulder, "But you can still go — Bryce will bring you to my house afterward. And I hope you and Bryce will have lots of fun. I'll stay up Friday night so you can tell me all about it when you get back to my house."

Katy considered telling Shelby she probably wouldn't be going with Bryce. Although he hadn't come right out and said he didn't want to take her after all, his behavior had done a good job of letting her know. It might make Shelby feel better to know Katy wasn't going either. Katy opened her mouth to share her own hurt, but Shelby interrupted.

"I'm really glad you're going, Katy. I hope you'll have a great time. I know Mennonites don't usually dance, and I hope it won't get you in trouble with your church or anything, but still ..." She sighed again, leaning on the desk and resting her chin in her hand. "At least I can be happy for you." A sad grin curved her lips. "You're kind of living a Cinderella story, you know? Getting to go to the ball with the handsome prince and all."

Katy swallowed the words she'd planned to say. Why make Shelby feel even worse? She glanced around, searching for Bryce. She found him on the back row in the corner — as far from her as he could possibly get. But to her surprise, he was looking right at her. And this time, when she met his eyes, he didn't turn away. He just looked at her, his face serious. Almost sad. Could he have possibly overheard what Shelby said?

The teacher said, "Miss Lambright?"

Katy spun to face the front. "Yes, Mr. Neelly?"

He waved a piece of note paper. "I've been instructed to send you to the gymnasium."

Katy frowned, confused.

Mr. Neelly raised his eyebrows. "Practice for homecoming — they need all of the royalty."

"Oh!" Katy jumped up and reached for her backpack.

"You can leave your things here. You'll be back before the bell rings," Mr. Neelly said.

A couple of kids snickered. Katy didn't even glance at them. But she couldn't help sneaking another quick look at Bryce. His eyes seemed to follow her out the door. Her heart pounding, she hurried toward the gym. She reached the big double doors at the same time as two older boys. Katy recognized one of them, Tony Adkins. She skidded to a stop, wanting them to go in ahead of her, but to her embarrassment, Tony swung one door open.

He winked and gestured for her to go in. "There ya go, cutie."

Katy ducked her head and scurried through the doorway. The two boys laughed. Katy considered turning around to tell them to knock it off. But instead she gathered her courage and flashed a quick smile over her shoulder. They laughed again, nudging each other. They were rude, but Katy didn't really care. The last laugh would be on them when she showed up Friday night looking like any other high school girl.

With a smile, Katy hurried over to join the others.

Chapter Sixteen

The senior girls all ignored me at practice today, and the freshman girl attendant didn't talk to anybody, including me. But the junior girl attendant, Adrianna Tolle, was really nice. I hope she's a candidate for queen next year and wins. Sometimes it seems like the nice people don't get the kind of recognition they deserve. Why is the popular crowd the mean crowd?

Katy paused and chewed the click cap on her pen as she considered what she'd just written. Then she put the pen to the notebook and clarified.

Not all of the popular kids are mean — Adrianna's popular and really nice — but the senior girls are all popular, and they weren't so nice. I wonder if being popular sometimes makes you think you're better than everybody else, so you end up treating others like they aren't important. If so, I don't ever want to be popular. I don't ever want to make someone feel as small and insignificant as those girls made me feel today.

Katy looked toward the closet. The doors were closed, but she envisioned the green dress on its hanger, waiting for her to wear it Friday night. Would those girls view her differently after they'd seen her in the green dress?

She turned back to her journal.

They had us write down our parents' names for the an-
nouncements. I started to put just Dad's name, but he'll
be married to Mrs. Graber—Rosemary—by then, so I
put Samuel and Rosemary Lambright *down for parents. I*
wanted to put my mom's name instead, but she's dead.

Katy's throat tightened. She swallowed and turned her focus to another topic.

I still don't know what to think about Bryce. He's never
said anything to me about my note. He still hasn't talked to
me at all. But today in history I caught him looking at me,
and during forensics I think he was going to talk to me, but
then Marlys (of course—she just can't leave him alone!)
grabbed his arm and dragged him off. I wonder what he
was going to say. Was he going to tell me he was sorry?
(OH, I HOPE SO!!!) Or was he going to say he couldn't take
me to homecoming after all? I wish I knew for sure.

She glanced at the clock. Dad would be done with the milking soon. She needed to hurry downstairs to finish supper, but she added one more line to her journal:

I also wish I could stop worrying that wearing Cora's
dress and getting all fixed up for homecoming is wrong.
It's just a dress, and it's just for one night. It doesn't
change who I am, does it?

Slamming the journal closed, Katy pushed out of her chair and clattered down the stairs. She finished grilling Swiss cheese and mushroom sandwiches just as Dad stepped through the door.

He sniffed the air. "Smells good."

Katy raised one shoulder in a feeble shrug. She hoped Dad wouldn't be upset about the simple supper. She'd spent too much time on her journal and hadn't had time to cook a full meal. Fortunately, Dad really liked the kind of sandwich she'd fixed. "I wanted to use up the last of the rye bread, so I grilled some sandwiches. We've got leftover salad from last night and half a blueberry pie."

"Well, it'll fill a stomach, and that's what matters," Dad said. "I guess it's good we're cleaning out the refrigerator since we'll all be gone this weekend." He waved toward the stairs. "I'll go wash up and then we can eat."

Katy placed the sandwiches—two for Dad, one for her—on plates, poured tall glasses of milk, then sat down and waited for Dad. He hustled in, plopped into his chair, and offered a prayer of thanks. Then he took a big bite of his sandwich. While he chewed, Katy cleared her throat.

"Dad?"

He looked at her, his eyebrows raised in silent query.

"Remember you told me I could decide about the homecoming ceremony and dance?"

Dad nodded.

Katy swallowed and made herself look straight into Dad's face. "I decided."

Dad put down his sandwich and fixed his gaze on her.

"I'm going to be the attendant. And I'm going to go to the homecoming game and dance. I don't know that I'm going with Bryce." She didn't explain why — she didn't think she could explain why. "And I won't stay at the dance for very long probably. There's a forensics meet on Saturday, so I can't be out too late. But I want to, you know, see what it's like. To be at the game with everybody and then go to a dance, I mean." She waited for Dad to frown or try to change her mind.

But his face didn't change. He bobbed his head in one slow nod. "All right, Katy-girl. Thank you for letting me know." He went back to eating.

Katy ate in silence, stunned by her dad's calm response to her announcement. He'd said he'd let her decide, but a part of her hadn't quite believed it. Now, however, she knew he intended to keep his word. The realization made her feel powerful and frightened both at once.

When they'd finished and Katy was clearing the table, someone knocked on the door. Dad opened it, and Katy heard him say, "Come on in, Annika."

Annika hurried in, and Dad snapped the door closed. He looked at Katy. "I've got some paperwork to do. I'll work at the dining room table so I won't be in your way." He left.

Without being asked, Annika picked up the remaining dishes on the table and carried them to the sink. She looked ready to burst with something. "Guess what?"

"Better just tell me," Katy said with a smile.

"Caleb asked me to the singing at the Pankratz place Friday night!"

Katy dropped the plate she was holding into the water-filled sink. Sudsy droplets spattered the front of her dress. She hissed, wishing she'd put on an apron before washing the dishes.

"Isn't it exciting? I thought he'd never ask me." Annika smiled so broadly her eyes crinkled up.

Katy swept the foamy dots from her front then plunged her hands back into the water. "It is exciting. I know it's what you wanted." But she realized she didn't sound very excited.

Annika must have recognized her lack of enthusiasm. "Is something wrong?" Annika glanced toward the dining room as if to make sure Dad wasn't listening, then she leaned close to Katy's ear. "You're not jealous, are you?"

Katy shot Annika a scowl. "Of course not! You know I don't like Caleb." She didn't like Caleb. She thought he was a pest. Yet the idea of him taking Annika to the singing bothered Katy. She just didn't know why it bothered her.

"Then couldn't you be just a little bit happy for me?" Annika's voice took on an edge. She snatched a salad bowl from the draining tray and rubbed a towel over it. "After all, you have all kinds of neat things happening at school. You're always going to tournaments or spending the night with your Salina friends. I'm always stuck here, cleaning my parents' house, cooking their dinners, and watching my little brothers and sisters. They won't even let me get a job so I can do something else. I deserve some fun."

"I hope you'll have fun," Katy said, and she meant it. But a little part of her still felt funny about Annika's announcement. Not so long ago, Caleb had told Katy he didn't want to give Annika ideas. Had he changed his mind? Or was he asking Annika in the hopes of making Katy jealous? According to Trisha, Cora, and Jewel, boys often paid attention to one girl as a means of gaining the attention of another girl.

Tony Adkins seemed to be using Jewel to get beer for a party. Jayden O'Connor tried to use Shelby for — Katy felt heat rush to her face — his pleasure. And now it seemed Caleb could be using Annika to make Katy jealous. But Annika wouldn't be happy if Katy shared that worry.

Katy said, "You'll have to tell me if going to a singing is more fun when you have a date, and — " She tipped sideways and peeked through the dining room doorway. Dad wasn't there. He must have gone upstairs for something. She finished, "I'll tell you if a high school dance is fun."

Annika's eyebrows shot high. "Dance? Are you really going to one?"

Katy nodded. "Dad said I could."

"Oh, Katy, the deacons will have a fit! You know how the fellowship feels about dancing."

"I know the fellowship frowns on it." Katy washed a plate and handed it to Annika. Maybe if she kept Annika's hands busy, Annika wouldn't be able to fuss too much. "But if Dad said I could go, the deacons can't be upset with me. Besides, it's only one dance. It isn't as if I'm going every weekend or something. And it's a school activity. All perfectly harmless."

"Even so . . ." Annika clicked her tongue on her teeth, reminding Katy of Aunt Rebecca. Now that Katy had told Annika, everyone would find out. Annika would tell her mom or older sister, and they'd tell someone else, and the whole fellowship would be in an uproar. Again.

Katy grabbed Annika's arm. Her wet fingers left a dark splotch on Annika's dress. "Can you maybe keep this a secret?"

"Why?" Annika's eyes narrowed. "Are you ashamed of it?"

Katy's ears grew hot. "Of course not!"

Annika gave Katy a skeptical look. "Are you sure? Usually people don't mind telling others about things they're proud of."

Katy knew Annika was right, and it compounded Katy's irritation. "I don't want you telling everyone, because it'll just cause problems. As I said, I'm not going to go to dances all the time. But this one is special."

"How so?" Annika sounded more curious than judgmental.

Katy shared, "It's homecoming—a really special time at the school—and I get to represent the sophomore class." She glanced again into the dining room. Dad had returned and sat hunched over a stack of papers. She lowered her voice to a whisper. "If you promise to keep quiet, I'll show you the dress I'm going to wear."

"Okay."

The girls quickly finished the dishes then bustled through the dining room. Dad looked up as they passed by. Katy said, "Annika and I are going up to my room for a while."

"Don't forget your homework," Dad said.

Katy never forgot her homework, but she said, "I won't." She closed the bedroom door even though Dad preferred she leave it open when she had guests. But she didn't want him coming up again and looking into her room while she was showing Annika the dress. She opened her closet door, and Annika crowded close behind Katy.

"Oh!" Annika let a little squeal. She reached past Katy and pulled out the orchid dress Mrs. Graber had sewn. "Is this for the wedding? My mom said Mrs. Graber chose beautiful colors." She scurried to the mirror and held the dress to her front. "Oh, I love this. I wish we wore the same size so I could borrow it sometime."

Katy stifled a giggle. Annika loved to eat, and her waistline showed it. There was no way Annika would be able to wear that dress. Katy crossed to the dresser and stood looking first at Annika's reflection and then her own in the mirror. Two Mennonite girls in white mesh caps with trailing white ribbons. Two faces clean of makeup and hair combed straight back. Two plain, unpretentious girls.

Just once, I want to be pretty. Just once.

Annika sighed and turned to push the dress into Katy's hands. "The dress I wore when I was Taryn's attendant wasn't nearly so pretty. I've never looked good in orange— I don't know why Taryn chose such an ugly color for her wedding. I'll never wear that dress again. But you could wear this one to singings and worship and even those speech tournaments for school. You're lucky to get to wear such a beautiful dress, Katy."

It took Katy a moment to remember Annika was talking about the wedding dress rather than the green dress. She took hold of Annika's arm and drew her back to the closet. "I want you to see the dress I'm wearing for homecoming." She hung the orchid dress in the closet and pulled the green dress free.

Annika's jaw dropped. She pinched the skirt between two fingers and held it out, her eyes following the line of sequins that decorated the sheer overlay. "You're really wearing this? Your dad said you could?"

Katy ignored the second question. "Yes, it's my home-coming dress."

"Wow!" Annika shook her head. "You know, Katy, you've always been a little different—bolder than the other girls. But I'd never have imagined you wearing something so ... daring."

"But isn't it pretty?" Katy touched one of the sections that formed the bodice. The sequins caught the light and sparkled like diamonds.

"It's pretty all right," Annika said, but she sounded grim.

"Want me to try it on for you?" Katy started to remove the dress from its hanger.

Annika held up both hands. "That's okay, Katy. I think it's better if you don't." She looked again at the dress, and for just a moment, Katy saw longing in Annika's eyes. A weak smile appeared on Annika's face. "We're not supposed to covet, remember?"

Katy giggled. Maybe she and Annika weren't so different after all.

Chapter Seventeen

Grampa Ben drove Katy to school early on Wednesday morning so she could attend the student Bible study. Even though none of the other kids in the group were Old Order Mennonite, two of them said they were Mennonite Brethren. There were also Baptist kids, Methodist kids, Presbyterian kids, Catholic kids, and three kids who attended an Assembly of God church. Katy had never heard of that denomination, but she assumed it was another Christian church, otherwise they wouldn't want to go to the Bible study.

She and Grampa Ben chatted on the drive in. They also laughed a lot. Katy always enjoyed time with her grandparents. All of her life, Grampa and Gramma Ruthie had been like another set of parents. Now that she attended school in Salina and had homework every evening, she didn't get to see them as often as she liked, so her time on Wednesday mornings with Grampa was special.

Katy stopped talking though while Grampa maneuvered his big black sedan through the Salina morning traffic. When they got to the city, his face always scrunched up in concentration. Driving in Salina was different than driving in little Schellberg. Katy didn't want to distract him. She wished she'd told Grampa about homecoming and getting to represent her class. The next time she'd see him would be at Dad and Mrs. Graber's wedding, and everyone's focus would be on the bride and groom. The way it should be.

Grampa pulled up to the curb and gave Katy a bright smile. "There you go, Katy-girl. Have a good day."

"I will," she said. She waved good-bye before dashing across the sidewalk and entering the school. Her steps slowed as she neared the classroom where the home economics teacher, Mrs. Parks, hosted the Bible study. Bryce attended the Bible study too. They'd sat together until he stopped talking to her. She didn't like all of the changes that had been forced on her lately, and she didn't like the anxious feeling that struck every time she might see Bryce. *Why couldn't things just be simple?*

Two girls came up beside her, and Katy moved aside so the girls could go on in. One of them paused and smiled at Katy. "Aren't you coming?" Katy drew in a deep breath and nodded. She followed the girls in. Bryce was already there, sitting at the far side of the circle beside a couple of boys. The chairs on his right side were empty. Katy paused again, looking at the empty chair next to Bryce, hoping he might pat the seat in invitation like he'd done at other times.

His hand didn't move. Katy sighed. Then Shelby bustled in and linked arms with Katy. "C'mon," she said, drawing Katy into the circle. "Let's sit." She tugged Katy across the room and flopped into a chair, leaving the one between herself and Bryce open. Katy looked once more at Bryce.

His face flushed red, and his gaze bounced all around the room as if he didn't know where to look. And for some reason, Katy decided not to avoid him. She turned and sat in the chair between him and Shelby.

Shelby giggled and nudged Katy with her elbow. She whispered, "You go, girl!"

Fire rushed from Katy's neck to her forehead, and she knew her face was beaming bright red, but she didn't care. She and Bryce could just sit there red-faced together. He was acting like an idiot, avoiding her instead of treating her the way he had before, and she wouldn't let him get away with it anymore. One of them had to be normal, so it might as well be her.

Mrs. Parks held her hand out to one of the older boys. "The floor is yours, Greg. What did you prepare for us this morning?"

The students took turns leading the study. The school rules said any kind of religious group had to be student led. Mrs. Parks attended so the study had an adult sponsor, but she never contributed. Katy noticed Mrs. Parks often smiled and nodded, though, offering approval of their discussions.

Greg held his open Bible in his hands and rested his elbows on his knees. "I'm gonna read the first part of Romans twelve." Bent forward with his head down, he read with a muffled voice, and Katy had to focus hard to hear. Even though he read from a different translation than the one Katy's church used, she recognized the verses. The leaders in her church had taught from Romans twelve more than once. She could recite some of the passage from the King James Version by memory. Verse two formed easily in her head. *"And be not conformed to this world: but be ye transformed by the renewing of your mind, that ye may prove what is that good, and acceptable, and perfect, will of God."*

Greg finished reading. Still hunched forward, he lifted his head slightly to look at the others. "I'm no preacher, but I think what the writer was trying to say is it's easy to get all caught up with stuff in the world and forget what we're all about. Christians are supposed to be all about pleasing God instead of ourselves. The stuff we think about the most—that's the stuff that becomes most important to us."

"I agree," a girl named Lily said. "I mean, it's like one of your friends gets the newest cell phone and all of a sudden your phone isn't good enough because you can't surf the Web *and* talk to somebody at the same time. Why is that so important?"

"'Cause the conversation might be boring—surfing the Web gives you something else to do," one of the boys quipped, and a few students chuckled.

Lily made a face. "You know what I'm trying to say. Sometimes we get all hung up on having the *newest* and *best* and then we can't be satisfied with anything because there's always something new and better out there somewhere. I think God wants us to be content with what we've got instead of always wanting more and better."

"Television commercials sure don't help," Shelby said as she sent a disgusted look around the circle. "Advertisers' main goal is to convince everybody they can't be happy unless they have the latest gadgets and name-brand clothes. It's ridiculous."

Brooke, the girl sitting next to Lily, slumped in her chair and folded her arms over her chest. "But what's wrong with wanting nice stuff? It's not a sin or anything to look nice or have nice things." She sounded a little defensive. Katy looked at Brooke's stylish clothes and the cool-looking cell phone resting in her lap. Brooke probably thought the others were picking on her.

Greg spoke again. "I don't think there's anything wrong with having nice things. That's not what I'm saying. Having stuff isn't the problem. Wanting stuff over wanting to please God is what's wrong."

"Yeah." Bryce squirmed, making the metal folding chair squeak. "Like the verse said, conform your thoughts to what God wants for you instead of what you want for yourself. Then you'll stay in His will." He shifted his head slightly, and his gaze met Katy's as he finished. "Maybe having new and best is God's will for you 'cause He knows you'll use it in good ways. And maybe *not* having new and best is God's will for you. But you have to figure that out before you start grabbing up all the stuff the media tries to tell you will make you happy."

Katy rarely contributed to the discussions, but she found herself adding, "Our elders teach us the only way anyone can find true contentment and joy is to serve God first, then others, and yourself last."

"That's really hard," Brooke said with a sigh.

Katy nodded. It was hard. When she'd spent all of her time in Schellberg, with only her family and fellowship members, she hadn't thought much about the things of the world. But now that she was spending her days with kids who owned lots of things, she found herself wondering what it was like to have a fun car like Shelby's or a cell phone like Brooke's. *And a sequined homecoming dress like the other girls.* She gulped, and her ears heated.

Mrs. Parks rose. "You've had a great discussion today, with lots to think about. Maybe we can have Greg read some more from Romans twelve next week?" She waited until Greg nodded. "But for now, we need to pray and then send you to your first-hour classes."

The kids all stood and held hands. Katy bowed her head, but she didn't really listen to Greg's prayer. She kept thinking about the good, acceptable, perfect will of God, and whether she wanted to follow God's will more than she wanted to be like the other girls in the school.

"Amen," Greg finished, and the circle broke apart. The kids became typical high school kids again, talking, laughing, and jostling each other as they poured into the hallway. Shelby and Katy got separated, and Katy found herself walking next to Bryce. Her tummy fluttered with nervousness, being so close to him after days of staying away from each other. She wondered if boys got tummy flutters too. She sneaked a glance at him and noticed his face looked a little red. Maybe his stomach was as trembly as hers.

She cleared her throat and braved a raspy whisper. "Did you get my note?"

He didn't look at her, but the red in his cheeks brightened. He nodded.

"Did it make you mad?"

He shook his head.

"Then why haven't you, you know, talked to me this week?"

Bryce stopped, so Katy did too. The kids behind them almost plowed into them. Grumbling, the others stepped around them. Bryce scooted over against the wall, and Katy followed. He set his lips in a fierce scowl. He'd said he wasn't mad. But at that moment, he looked very angry.

"I guess I was mad," he admitted, "but not at you. At myself. For being so stupid."

Katy tipped her head, waiting for him to continue. Other kids flowed past them, their voices jumbling together into a mindless clamor of noise.

"When I asked you to go to homecoming with me —" He paused and swallowed.

Suddenly Katy knew what he meant by being stupid. He hadn't been stupid to ignore her; he'd been stupid to ask her out in the first place. Her nose and eyes began to sting, and she quickly backed away. "I have to get to class."

"Katy, wait!"

She heard Bryce's call, but she darted between other students. Ignoring their protests, she hurried on, determined to escape Bryce and the stabbing pain in her heart. She left Bryce behind, but the hurt stayed with her.

Chapter Eighteen

Katy made sure she didn't look around the rooms during her morning classes. She didn't want to accidentally make eye contact with Bryce. She avoided him in the hallway by rushing out of the room before anybody else, and she kept her face aimed straight ahead. By lunch she felt — borrowing one of Gramma Ruthie's expressions — like a wrung-out mop. She got her tray and fell into her seat at the table with Cora and Trisha. They took one look at her and both exclaimed, "What is *wrong* with you?"

Hearing them speak in unison with exactly the same vocal inflection should have been hilarious. Katy wished she could laugh. But she couldn't manage even a little giggle. She sighed and told them the truth. "Bryce told me he'd been stupid to ask me to the dance."

"Oh, Katy," they chorused. Cora reached across the table to pat Katy's wrist. Trisha sat looking at her in sympathy. Katy appreciated their kindness, but it didn't erase the pain Bryce had inflicted.

"Yeah. Stupid. *Stupid* to be with me. Just stupid." Katy repeated the words even though saying them was like rubbing salt in a wound. But for some reason, she had to say it again and again. "I mean, what boy with any sense at all would want to go out with 'the little Amish girl'?"

"You aren't Amish," Cora said.

Trisha released a huff. "She knows that. But I've heard the kids call her Amish. I think they do it to be rude." She looked at Katy. "Don't let Bryce bother you, Katy. He's stupid, all right, for being such a ... a *boy*." She made *boy* sound like a dirty word. "As for homecoming, you just wait. Lots of kids go without dates. And when you show up in Cora's dress, your hair all done up and everything, every boy in the school will want to ask you out on a date. Katy, you really are a knockout in that dress."

Cora nodded enthusiastically. "Oh, yeah, and then Bryce'll kick himself for being such a jerk." She waggled her eyebrows, smirking impishly. "Of course, it'll be too late, 'cause you'll be having a blast with all the other guys."

Katy sniffed. "You think so?"

"I *know* so," Trisha said. "I mean it, last Saturday when you put that dress on — " She and Cora exchanged a quick look. "We talked about it all the way back to Salina. Even Jewel said she couldn't believe the transformation, and you know how hard it is to coax a compliment out of her." Trisha grinned. "Girlfriend, you are going to knock everyone's socks off!"

Throughout the afternoon, Katy had a hard time paying attention to her teachers. So many thoughts tumbled in her mind she could hardly keep them straight. The verse from Romans about not conforming to the world slammed against Cora and Trisha's exclamation that Bryce would kick himself when he saw her in the emerald dress. Then that thought got knocked aside by a wave of hurt — Bryce thought being with her was stupid. *Stupid, stupid, stupid. Being stupid is even worse than being weird.* Katy wanted to forget what Bryce had said — even forget that she'd ever liked him — but she couldn't. How does a person turn off feelings? Impossible.

Last hour arrived, and even though Katy felt sick to her stomach, she knew she couldn't skip forensics again. They had a tournament, and she needed to practice. She'd just have to do what she'd done all day and not look at Bryce. It was harder in forensics, but she could do it if she made up her mind. Hadn't Aunt Rebecca told her from the time Katy was little that Katy had the hardest head of any of the Lambrights? Aunt Rebecca hadn't meant it as a compliment, but Dad said being hardheaded could be a good thing if a person set her head in the right direction.

So I can manage to look past Bryce — the same way he's been looking past me all week. Two can play the game as easily as one. She entered the forensics classroom with her chin high and her shoulders square.

Mr. Gorsky greeted her with a smile. "Kathleen, I'm glad to see you're feeling better."

"Yes, sir, I am," she said, trying to mean it.

"Would you like to present first today since you missed the chance to perform on Monday?"

Katy's stomach began to whirl, but she swallowed hard and nodded. "Sure. No problem."

When everyone settled into their seats, Katy stepped to the front of the classroom. *Performance mode*, she reminded herself. She clasped her hands behind her back, looked straight at her audience — and locked eyes with

Bryce. "I-into every ... every life—" She gulped. She couldn't remember her speech.

After a few uncomfortable seconds of silence, Mr. Gorsky cleared his throat. "Kathleen?"

She jerked to look at her teacher.

"Would you like to start again?"

She nodded.

"All right. Take a deep breath, gather your thoughts. You'll be fine."

Katy did exactly as her teacher directed. She closed her eyes briefly, drew in a mighty breath, and formed the speech in her head. When she opened her eyes again, she made sure her face was pointed away from Bryce. This time her speech flowed without any problems. The others applauded, the way they always did when someone finished. The applause for the popular kids was always more enthusiastic, but Katy tried not to let it bother her.

"Critiques," Mr. Gorsky said, stepping up beside Katy. Several kids put their hands in the air, and Mr. Gorsky began calling names so they could share their thoughts on Katy's presentation. Katy listened politely, agreeing with some of the comments and disagreeing with others. She didn't always make the changes her classmates suggested, but she always did what Mr. Gorsky instructed. He knew better than anyone else.

"All right, last comment," Mr. Gorsky said. "Bryce."

Katy's pulse sped up. If Bryce criticized her, her hard-headedness might not be strong enough to hold her heart together.

"I just wanted to say Katy does a good job of making eye contact with the audience. When she presents, it's like she's just sitting and talking directly to you, so her speech is very engaging."

Bryce used words that Mr. Gorsky had used in the past. Katy didn't want Bryce's comments to mean more than her teacher's did, but a part of the irritation she had carried all day melted with Bryce's compliment. Her gaze locked on Bryce's solemn face. "Thank you." Then she glanced across the others in the room so they would know she meant them too.

She became an audience member and watched the other students. Her chest got tight and achy when Bryce and Marlys performed their duet act. Maybe she'd tell Mr. Gorsky she'd like to do a duet act next year—it looked like fun. But maybe it only looked fun because Bryce and Marlys worked so well together. Katy hated to admit it because she really didn't care much for Marlys, but their act was better than the other pair of students who did duet acting.

At the end of the hour, Mr. Gorsky said, "Remember we won't have class tomorrow because of the homecoming assembly."

Marlys sent a disdainful look around the classroom. "It is too weird having the assembly on Thursday instead of game day. Who scheduled a speaker on *homecoming day*?"

Katy stared at Marlys in amazement. The Kansas State Treasurer was making a special visit to their school, and Marlys wanted to complain about it? Katy could hardly wait to hear the man's presentation.

Mr. Gorsky raised one eyebrow. "When hosting special visitors, we sometimes have to fit our schedules around theirs, Marlys."

Marlys rolled her eyes.

Mr. Gorsky cleared his throat and went on. "Since the assembly is tomorrow, we have only one more practice before we leave Saturday. Some of you—" He looked directly at a boy who had forgotten a whole section of his presentation, "—should review at home as well." Then he smiled. "But for the most part, we're ready, and I look forward to a good meet. I'll see you Friday."

The class gathered up their things with the usual chatter. Katy retrieved her backpack and turned toward the door. Bryce stepped into her pathway. "Can I talk to you for a minute?"

"I don't think there's anything left to say, Bryce." She didn't know how she found the courage, but she spoke honestly and openly. "I was so excited when you asked me to homecoming because I liked you and I thought we could have fun. But like I wrote in my note, then you changed. I want to be friends, but friends don't ignore each other one day and talk to each other the next. It's too confusing. I told you to decide whether to be my friend or not, and you kept ignoring me. So I guess you made your choice. I'm sorry it worked out that way—I really hoped ... hoped ..."

Her bravery faded as disappointment welled up and threatened to emerge as tears. She sniffed hard and made herself finish. "I hoped you'd choose to be my friend, but friendship can't be forced. So ..."

"But, Katy, I wanted to say—"

She shook her head. "I have to go. It's my dad's wedding rehearsal tonight, and I can't miss the bus. 'Bye, Bryce."

She dashed away, wishing her last words hadn't sounded so final.

The wedding rehearsal reminded Katy of the homecoming rehearsal. A lot of talking about what everyone should do followed by walking in and standing for a long time, listening to more talk, then finally getting to sit down. The other thing the two practices had in common was very few people paid any attention to Katy. She understood that her dad and Mrs. Graber were the most important people and everyone should be focusing on them, but she couldn't help feeling a little left out. She was an attendant after all.

Mrs. Graber's daughter lived in Ohio, and she couldn't come to the wedding because she was expecting a baby and her husband didn't want her so far from home. If she'd come, she would've been the attendant instead of Katy. Katy felt bad that Mrs. Graber's daughter wasn't there, but Katy did appreciate having an important role in the wedding. Both of Mrs. Graber's sons had driven over from Meschke. Katy was shocked at how tall and handsome they both were. She felt a little tongue-tied in their presence.

The oldest one escorted Mrs. Graber down the aisle and "gave" her to Dad. Katy got a lump in her throat when she watched the rehearsal. There was something in Dad's eyes as he took Mrs. Graber's hand, a tenderness Katy had never seen there before. Had he looked at Katy's mother in the same way when they married? Katy supposed she shouldn't be thinking about her mother during her dad's wedding rehearsal with someone else, but she couldn't seem to help it.

Uncle Albert served as Dad's groomsman, so he escorted Katy up and down the aisle. Uncle Albert stuck his elbow straight out for Katy to grab and pursed his face into a funny, overly serious expression that made Katy laugh. Uncle Albert was the opposite of Dad, who was rarely playful. Katy appreciated Uncle Albert's silly antics during the practice. They helped take her mind off of her worries.

The church ladies had prepared a meal for the wedding party. When they finished rehearsing, they all went to the church basement to eat. The elder who would be performing the ceremony, Dad and Mrs. Graber, Mrs. Graber's family members, Gramma Ruthie, and Grampa Ben sat at one table. There wasn't a seat available for Katy. So Dad asked her to sit with Aunt Rebecca, Uncle Albert, and their kids.

Katy went without complaining, but she wasn't happy. Much of the time Katy didn't enjoy being around her cousins. Uncle Albert and Aunt Rebecca had five children, including fourteen-year-old twins. Since the twins were close to Katy's age, they should have been able to be good friends. But Lola and Lori had never seemed to need anybody else since they had each other. Besides, they were a lot like their mother — too critical. So they weren't always very much fun.

As soon as Katy sat down, Lori nudged her arm. "Mom says Uncle Samuel says you're staying in Salina for the weekend while Uncle Samuel and Aunt Rosemary take a short trip."

How odd that her cousins already referred to Mrs. Graber as Aunt Rosemary when Katy still stumbled over calling the woman by her first name. She poked her fork into the broccoli, bacon, and onion salad on her plate. "That's right."

Lola leaned in from the other side. "And you're going to a homecoming. But Mom didn't know what that meant."

Katy wished Dad wouldn't tell Aunt Rebecca everything. She told the twins, and somehow Lola and Lori always managed to make everything Katy did seem wrong. Without going into too much detail, she explained the purpose of homecoming.

"So it's just a basketball game with extra people there?" Lori made a face. "What's so special that you have to go? Mom said you could've stayed with us except for homecoming."

Katy wouldn't have wanted to stay with Aunt Rebecca. If she'd stayed with anyone, it would have been her grandparents. But she didn't mention that to the twins. She said, "It's special because they crown a king and queen. Each class has representatives who sit on the royal court." Katy tried to look humble as she added, "And I'm the representative for my class."

"You?" Lola gawked, her mouth hanging open. "Why'd they pick you?"

Katy wasn't about to tell Lori and Lola she'd been chosen as a joke. She shrugged.

"I guess that's a good reason to go," Lori acknowledged.

"I also have a forensics tournament on Saturday, so it's easier if I'm just in Salina."

"That makes sense," Lola said. "But you're staying home tomorrow, right? How can you go to school when you've got the wedding and everything tomorrow evening?"

Katy hadn't thought about needing to miss school for the wedding. But Lola was right—the wedding ceremony would start at six o'clock, and Deacon Pauls advised them to be at the church an hour earlier. Katy didn't get home from school until almost four thirty. She would need to stay home.

Which meant she wouldn't be there for the homecoming assembly. Michael Evans would walk in alone. The seniors would think their prank worked. Katy's lips twitched as she fought a grin. But they'd all be surprised when she showed up for the homecoming game and walked in with Michael.

Lola poked Katy on the arm. "What's so funny?"

Katy looked at her.

"You're sitting there smiling like someone told a joke."

Katy shook her head. "Nothing." She pretended great interest in picking the bacon pieces from the broccoli salad.

After a moment, Lola went back to eating, letting the question go unanswered. There was a joke coming, all right, and Katy wouldn't be the butt of it—she'd be the instigator. She ignored the little pinch in her conscience and put a bite of salad in her mouth.

Chapter Nineteen

Because Katy didn't have to get up to meet the school bus on Thursday, Dad told her she could sleep in. But she awakened early anyway. Her body didn't seem to understand days off. She heard Dad rustling around, so she pulled on her robe over her nightgown and stepped across the landing to tap on his door.

The door popped open. Dad was dressed, but he hadn't combed his hair or shaved yet. He looked so rumpled, Katy had to swallow a giggle. "What're you doing up?" he asked.

"I thought I'd offer to milk for you this morning."

His eyebrows rose.

She shrugged. "Consider it a wedding present." She hadn't gotten Dad anything else — what kind of gift did you give a couple who already had all the household items they needed?

Dad's face broke into a huge smile. "That's a super gift, Katy-girl. Thank you." He tugged her against his chest for a rare hug then released her. He glanced at his wristwatch. "Caleb will be here in another twenty minutes — better get yourself dressed."

Katy dashed for her bedroom, calling over her shoulder, "I'll fix breakfast after we're done with the milking, so just relax, Dad!" Amazing how good it felt to give a little something extra to Dad this morning.

Caleb arrived at six o'clock, right on schedule, and Katy immediately gave the truck's horn a push to call in the cows. Caleb sent her a curious look as she bustled for the milk room. "Sure didn't expect to see you this morning. How come you're milking again? Is your dad sick or something?"

"No, just gave him the morning off since it's his wedding day. C'mon, let's get started. I've got lots to do today."

Caleb shrugged and followed her in. He opened the doors, and cows entered on cue. Even though Katy hadn't intended to talk to Caleb while they milked, a question rolled around in the back of her mind and finally she had to let it out.

She hollered over the noisy machines, "Annika said you're taking her to the singing tomorrow night."

Caleb didn't look up from removing the suction cups, but she saw his head bob in agreement.

"But you told me taking her would give her ideas. Why'd you change your mind?"

Caleb gave the cow a smack on its hindquarters, and it wandered out of the room. He waited for the next cow to move into position and attached the suction cups before answering. "Didn't want to go alone."

Katy frowned at him. Her cow was finished, so she quickly released it and got another one ready before speaking again. "You shouldn't invite her if you really don't like her, Caleb. She likes you. You'll end up hurting her if you're just asking her so you don't have to go alone and she thinks it's a real date." It hurt her throat to yell over the loud machines, but she didn't care. Caleb needed to use better sense.

He looked at her over the machines, his face innocent. "It's a real date."

"Are you sure? Because you just said you didn't want to go alone."

"I only said that so you wouldn't feel bad."

Katy frowned. "That doesn't make sense."

He shrugged. "Well, I didn't want you feeling like you got left out or something, so I said something stupid."

Boys seem to say a lot of stupid things, Katy's thoughts groused.

Caleb went on. "But really, Annika's okay even if she is a little pushy. I don't mind going with her."

Katy decided not to talk anymore. It was too hard to be heard over the machines. But she would be watching Caleb and Annika at the wedding — they would be there, because everyone in Schellberg always came to the weddings. If she thought he might end up doing something that would hurt Annika, she'd jump on him so fast he wouldn't know what had hit him. The idea made her smile.

When the milking was done, Katy left Caleb to clean the milk room and feed the cows while she hurried back to the house to fix breakfast. Dad hadn't come downstairs yet, so she took her time preparing waffles with cinnamon and chopped pecans, fried eggs, and crisp bacon. Her stomach growled in anticipation, and she could hardly wait to eat. Dad expressed his appreciation for the wonderful breakfast, which made Katy's heart lift. After today, Katy wouldn't have to fix every meal. Mrs. Graber—Rosemary—would get the compliments. So Katy was glad she'd gone to so much trouble today and could savor Dad's praises.

Dad finished eating and pushed aside his plate. "Katy-girl, I need to go over to the church to put up the arbor and help set up tables in the basement. The ladies will be there around noon to do the decorating. Do you want to come with me, or do you need to stay here and do some schoolwork?"

She had schoolwork to do, but she really wanted to be with Dad. She sighed. "I'd better do my assignments. But I want to help with the decorating, so can you take me to the church this afternoon?"

Dad nodded, pushing away from the table. "That'd be fine. I'm sure Rosemary will want you there too. Plan on taking your wedding clothes with you and dressing there with Rosemary." He grabbed his jacket from the peg by the back door and hurried out.

By the time he returned at eleven thirty, Katy had finished her homework, packed her wedding clothes including a pair of white sandals and some flesh-toned hose, and fixed a light lunch of canned tomato soup and cheese sandwiches. Dad grinned when he saw the sandwiches and soup.

"Smart girl. We'll want to be good and hungry at suppertime with all the food Rosemary and the ladies have prepared for the wedding supper—it'll be a feast." He blessed the food, and they ate in silence. Dad seemed to be lost in thought, and Katy decided not to disturb him even though she wished they would talk during their last meal with just the two of them.

"Leave the dishes in the sink—there's not enough to bother with," Dad said when the soup and sandwiches were gone. "I'll get you over to the church. Do you have everything?"

Katy nodded.

"Are you sure? You won't be coming back to the house again."

Katy sighed. "I'm sure, Dad."

Dad grinned and gave her shoulders a squeeze. "I'm sorry. I keep forgetting you aren't a little girl anymore. I should trust you to know what you need to do."

Dad's confidence in her should have warmed her, but instead, a prickle of unease wiggled through Katy's middle. She hoped Dad's trust wasn't misplaced. She grabbed the bag she'd packed and said, "Let's go."

Dad dropped Katy off in the churchyard, and she dashed past the row of vehicles lining the south side of the church. The others had obviously all arrived, and they'd be working without her. She clattered into the cloakroom but slowed her pace before entering the worship room. She knew better than to run into the room where they worshiped as a congregation.

As soon as she came in, Caleb's mother spotted her. She smiled and gestured Katy over. "Oh, good, I can use your creative hands, Katy. My clumsy fingers refuse to tie a pretty bow."

Katy eagerly assisted Mrs. Penner in attaching decorations formed of silk orchids, ivy, and wide brown ribbon to the end of each bench. Arrangements with the same silk flowers and greenery in tall, cut-glass vases graced the windowsills. Katy paused for a moment to admire the

display. She loved the colors Rosemary had chosen for the
wedding: soft orchid, mint green, and a color the bride
had called old willow, but Katy thought it looked like milk
chocolate. The two pale colors, accented with the rich
shade of brown, blended perfectly.

"It's so pretty in here," Katy commented as she leaned
down to fluff a bow.

Mrs. Penner nodded in agreement, the black ribbons
of her cap bouncing on her shoulders. "Have you seen the
bouquets yet? They're lovely." She winked. "I'm almost
envious that I wasn't chosen to be the attendant so I could
take the bouquet home with me."

"Are they here?"

Mrs. Penner laughed. "In a box in the cloakroom. Go
peek."

Katy grinned in thanks and hurried to the cloakroom.
Two white boxes, each large enough to hold a three-layer
cake, rested on a table in the corner. Katy lifted the lid on
the first one. She knew at once it was Rosemary's. Her eyes
roved over the cluster of snow-white rosebuds with a few
pinkish baby orchids tucked in between. Narrow silk ribbons in brown and mint held the bouquet to a white Bible.

For a moment, Katy's chin quivered. The Bible her
mother had carried on her wedding day eighteen years
ago, covered in dried roses and tied with faded pink ribbon, sat in the trunk Katy had shoved into the corner of
her room. She closed her eyes, fighting tears, as images of
the two bouquets—one fresh and new, one withered and
worn—fought for prominence in her mind.

*Mom, why did you leave us? Your wedding day must
have been just as beautiful as Rosemary's. You must have*

been just as happy on that day. Why did it change? Katy's questions went unanswered, because the only person who knew the answers was gone.

"What do you think?"

Mrs. Penner's voice startled Katy. She spun around and pressed her hand to her chest. The woman pursed her face. "Oh, I'm sorry—did I startle you?" She hurried forward and touched Katy's arm.

Katy managed a wobbly smile. "It's okay. I was just thinking about something, and—" She bit down on her lip. She wouldn't talk about her mother. Not to anyone. She replaced the lid. "The bride's bouquet is beautiful."

"Well, look at yours—it's just as lovely."

But Katy decided she didn't want to see it just yet. She turned toward the door leading to the worship room. "I'll let it be a surprise. Let's finish decorating so we can go downstairs and help with the tables."

Mrs. Penner gave her a funny look, but she didn't argue. They hung the remaining swags then wove ivy, silk orchids, and brown ribbon on the white trellis Dad had built as an arbor. When they were finished, the worship room was more beautiful than Katy had ever seen it. She looked around, amazed by the transformation in the simple room.

Mrs. Penner must have understood Katy's awe. She slipped her arm around Katy's shoulders. "If you think it's beautiful now, wait until we light the candles."

Katy nodded, imagining the room under candle glow. Tears again pricked her eyes, but she didn't know why.

Mrs. Penner gave her another squeeze. "C'mon, Katy. Let's head downstairs. You haven't even said hello to

Rosemary yet." She paused, her face pensive. "You know, Katy, you're very blessed."

Katy tipped her head. "Why?"

"Your father is marrying a woman who has a tender heart for you. She already loves you and thinks of you as her daughter." Mrs. Penner laughed softly. "I think she's as excited about raising another girl as she is about becoming a wife again." Mrs. Penner pushed Katy's ribbon over her shoulder and sighed. "Some stepmothers see their husband's children as an intrusion."

Hurt flashed in the woman's eyes, and Katy wondered what memories rushed through Mrs. Penner's mind in that moment. But then Mrs. Penner smiled and gave Katy's shoulder a pat. "But you won't ever have to feel like an unwelcome intrusion with Rosemary. She truly wants to be a mother to you. I hope you'll be grateful, and you'll let her mother you just a little. After all, it's important for a girl to have a mother."

Katy nodded solemnly. *I just wish I could have my real one instead of a substitute.*

Dad's wedding flowed perfectly from the processional to the recessional. Katy battled a mighty lump in her throat when she listened to her dad and Rosemary recite their vows of commitment and charity to one another. Katy's chest ached in a beautiful way, and she felt blessed to be able to witness the ceremony that bound her father to Rosemary.

They turned to face the congregation as Deacon Pauls pronounced them Mr. and Mrs. Lambright. Katy gulped several times, trying not to cry. Dad glowed with happiness and Rosemary beamed, just the way a groom and bride should look on their wedding day. And even though Katy still wished her own mother hadn't left, Katy was happy for her dad. He deserved to be loved and cherished by a woman like Rosemary.

The congregation followed the wedding party to the basement, and this time Katy got to sit at the main table with her dad, new stepmother, and Uncle Albert. The food was plentiful and delicious, and Katy ate until her stomach ached. But some of the ache was from laughing so much. Uncle Albert kept telling Rosemary funny stories about Dad when he was growing up — things Katy had never heard before — and it pleased Katy to know Dad had been an ornery boy who got into his share of trouble. Maybe she was more like Dad than she had imagined.

Even after the plates were empty, people sat around and talked, enjoying the time of fellowship. Annika pulled a chair next to Katy and leaned close so they could hear each other. "Katy, you looked so beautiful tonight! Like a princess."

Who else had told Katy she was like a princess? *Oh, yes, Shelby.* But Shelby had meant she looked princess-like in the emerald dress. Katy smoothed her hands down the sheeny bodice of her caped orchid dress. "Thank you. I kind of felt like one, too, in my new dress with my bouquet." She touched the cascading bouquet of orchids, pale peach rosebuds, and abundant ivy. "I'm glad Rosemary decided to use silk flowers. They'll keep forever and still look nice." *Unlike the bouquet in my trunk.* Katy pushed that image aside. This was not a time to think about the past!

Annika giggled. "Maybe you can carry it tomorrow night at the homecoming ceremony. It blends so perfectly with your dress."

Katy looked at the bouquet again. The ivy did hold narrow veins of emerald green on the paler leaves. She smiled. "You're right. It does match. Maybe I will."

"I wish I could be there to see you walk in but—" Annika sneaked a glance around the room. Her lips curved when she found Caleb. "I'll be busy."

Katy placed her hand on Annika's arm. "Annika, will you do me a favor?"

Annika pulled her gaze away from Caleb and looked at Katy. "Sure. What?"

"Don't get too hung up on Caleb, okay?" Annika's brows pulled down, but Katy went on. "I know he's the only boy our age in Schellberg, but don't like him just because he's, I don't know, available. God has a husband all picked out for you. It might be Caleb, and it might not be. So wait until you know for sure before you ... well ... love him."

Annika's face turned bright red. "*Love* him?" She flapped her hands in front of her face, as if needing to cool off. "Katy, I'm not ready to *love* anybody. You think I want my own house and all the responsibility already?" She blasted a huff of breath and shook her head. "No, I just wanna have some fun. A date. And I like him enough to date him." She flashed a flirtatious smirk in Caleb's direction. "But I'm not serious about him. Not yet."

Katy wasn't sure whether she was irritated or assured by Annika's answer, but she decided to drop the subject. They talked about other, lighthearted things, and at nine o'clock Deacon Pauls announced that it was time to send the bride and groom into their new life as husband and wife.

Katy pushed away from the table and turned to face her dad and stepmother. Dad put his arm around Rosemary's waist and pulled her close. He smiled at Katy. "Well, Katy-girl, are you ready to go home?"

From now on Rosemary would always be in Katy's house. An odd feeling, almost of panic, fluttered through Katy's chest. But she forced her lips into a smile and said, "Sure, Dad . . . and Rosemary. Let's go."

Dad held out his other arm, and Katy scurried to his side. They walked out together with the congregation following. Their cries of congratulations, good wishes, and God's blessings filled Katy's ears so thoroughly that the phrases continued to ring through her dreams.

Chapter Twenty

Katy entered the kitchen Friday morning to find Rosemary putting breakfast on the table. Katy came to a halt right inside the door and stared at the neatly set table, platters of sausage, eggs, and toast, and glasses of milk. She shook her head.

"You don't like sausage and eggs?"

Rosemary's dismayed voice pulled Katy's attention to the woman. "No, I love what you fixed. But it's the day after your wedding. You shouldn't be doing any work. I could've cooked."

Rosemary laughed, her eyes crinkling. "Now, I'm not going to use something like a wedding as an excuse to be lazy." She moved to the stove and lifted the coffee percolator. "Besides, I'll have all morning to pack for our trip. You need to do that before you leave for school."

Katy walked to the table and slid into the chair she always sat in. "I'm already packed." She'd put everything she needed in a suitcase when they returned from church last night. The emerald dress was folded as neatly as possible and nestled in the middle of her other clothes. She hoped it wouldn't wrinkle.

"Well, good." Rosemary poured a cup of coffee for herself then set the percolator on the table. "I bet you're excited. Your dad told me about all the fun things happening this weekend. It sounds as if you'll stay very busy but have lots of fun while we're away."

Katy didn't know how to respond. Dad was so quiet in the mornings. Although it was kind of nice to have someone chatty and cheerful to start the day with, it wasn't Katy's routine yet. It would take time for her to adjust to the change.

Rosemary continued. "Your dad said he might be late coming in, so go ahead and eat while it's hot. But may I join you?"

"You'd rather eat with me than with Dad?" Katy stared at her stepmother in surprise.

A laugh rang — this woman laughed more often than anyone else Katy knew. "I'd rather have a hot breakfast than a cold one, yes."

Katy grinned. Rosemary sat down across from Katy and held out her hand. "Would you like to offer grace, or should I?"

Katy hesitantly placed her hand in Rosemary's. Her warm, soft palm felt very different than Dad's calloused hand, but it offered a sense of security Katy didn't understand. She said, "You, please." She listened to Rosemary's simple prayer, and then they ate. The eggs were perfect — over medium, the way Katy liked them — and the toast lightly browned. Rosemary did know how to cook.

While they ate, they visited. Katy held back at first, unsure and a little uncomfortable, but as the minutes slipped by she allowed herself to relax. Mrs. Penner's comments about Rosemary not seeing Katy as an intrusive presence were proved true during their first breakfast together as stepmother and stepdaughter. Katy believed Rosemary truly liked her and wanted to spend time with her. The thought warmed her.

As they finished, Rosemary said, "I have to admit, Kathleen, it's wonderful to be able to settle in here and call Schellberg home. It's a welcoming community, and I feel so accepted even though I didn't grow up here." A smile curved her lips. "I almost envy you, having had the privilege of being born and raised in the same town. My father had a restless soul, and he moved us several times when I was growing up, so I never felt completely secure. Rather like a misfit, I suppose."

Katy blinked several times, surprised. Rosemary had eased into Schellberg so effortlessly, Katy would never have imagined Rosemary feeling any uncertainty.

Rosemary continued, almost as if she were talking to herself. "But you're a part of three generations who have called Schellberg home — your grandparents, your father, and you. It must give you a true sense of homecoming every time you drive through the center of town, visit your grandparents' house, or attend a worship service." Suddenly she shook her head, releasing an embarrassed chuckle. "And listen to me, going on and on. I suppose I've had too many years alone. It's nice to have someone to talk to again. You might have to tell me to be quiet!"

Katy shook her head. "No. I liked hearing what you said. And you're right — I have been very fortunate." *If my mother had taken me away with her, what kind of life would I have had? Not the one I've been given, that's for sure.*

Dad popped open the back door and stuck his head in. "Katy-girl? You ready? I need to take you to the bus stop."

Katy bounced up. "Yes."

Rosemary rose too, looking at Katy. "Do you mind if I ride along to the bus stop? I'd like to see you off since we won't see you again for a few days."

Warmth flooded Katy. A sweet, tender feeling of acceptance. *This is homecoming — for Rosemary and for me.* Katy nodded. "That's fine."

"Thank you." Rosemary headed for the pegs, where her coat hung next to Katy's.

Katy backed up toward the stairs. "I'll be out in a minute. Annika said I should carry my wedding bouquet for homecoming, but I forgot to pack it."

Dad frowned at his wristwatch. "I don't want you to miss the bus."

"Don't worry — I won't be late!" Katy raced toward the stairs.

A celebratory spirit permeated the school's homecoming day. Kids broke into spontaneous cheers between classes, they chanted fight songs in the cafeteria, and no one was reprimanded for cutting up in class. Even teachers who never joked or laughed were more relaxed on homecoming day. At the end of last hour, everyone burst through the doors, eager to begin the game and festivities.

Katy and Shelby hurried toward Shelby's Beetle, but someone called Shelby's name. The girls paused. Jayden O'Connor trotted up to them. He glanced at Katy. "Hey, mind if I talk to Shelby alone?"

Katy looked at Shelby. Shelby said, "It's okay." So Katy carried her suitcase and backpack to the car and waited. She tried not to stare, but she couldn't deny curiosity. Jayden stood with his thumbs caught in his jeans pockets, shifting from foot to foot like he was nervous, and Shelby folded her arms over her chest in a defensive pose. They didn't talk long, and Shelby turned and ran to the car. Before Katy could ask what he'd wanted, Shelby said, "Can you believe it? He asked me to go to the dance with him again — as friends."

Katy's mouth dropped open. "Are you going?"

"No." Shelby snorted. "As if I'd go just so he doesn't have to show up without a date." Then she shrugged. "But I think I'll go after all — with Cora and Trisha. And I might dance with him — if he asks." A shy grin creased her face. "Jayden really is a pretty decent guy. But he needs to understand I'm not gonna play games. He can't take advantage of me, you know what I mean?"

Katy thought she did. She nodded.

Shelby frowned toward the school. "I wonder where Jewel is. We need to get to the house, or we won't have time to get all spruced up before the game."

"Want me to go look for her?" Katy thought she'd spotted Jewel near the senior lockers as they were walking out. She was probably talking to Tony again.

"Well ..." Shelby looked uncertain.

Katy started for the school. "I think I know where to find her — I'll be right back." She wriggled her way through the groups of students who mingled on the lawn to chat. The hallways were nearly empty, though, and she had no trouble wending her way to the senior lockers. The moment she turned the corner, she spotted Jewel and Tony leaning against the lockers. Jewel had her back to Katy. She opened her mouth to call Jewel's name, but before she could speak, Tony pushed off the lockers and said, "See ya around, kid." He ambled away, but Jewel didn't move.

Katy took two steps toward Jewel. Only then did she notice Jewel's shoulders shaking. Soft sobs reached Katy's ears. Concerned, Katy dashed to face Jewel. "Jewel, what's wrong?"

"He's a jerk. Just a total jerk." Jewel blasted the words through her tears. "I can't believe he only spent time with me to get — to get — " She didn't finish the sentence, and she looked up and down the hallway with her face scrunched tightly. "I'm just so mad at myself for not seeing the truth."

Katy wanted to put her arm around Jewel's shoulder and offer comfort, but she was certain Jewel would push her away. So she stood silent and helpless.

Jewel slammed her hand against the locker door. "I believed him when he said he liked me. When he said we could go the dance if I'd help him out for the party afterward. I should've known someone like him wouldn't really like someone like me." Her voice carried a deep hurt that pierced Katy. "I just wanted to be with the popular kids. You know, to be popular too."

Katy touched Jewel's arm. "I know how you feel. Sometimes I want that too. But — " She swallowed, accepting the truth. "Doing things just to make somebody else happy — things that go against your own conscience — will never make you happy. You have to think about what God wants for you instead."

Jewel rolled her eyes. "Don't go getting all religious on me. You know I don't believe that stuff." She wiped away the tears, leaving black mascara smudges below her eyes. A wobbly, sad smile appeared on her face. "We better go before the principal throws us out. But we'll be back tonight, right? Can't let Jerk Tony keep me from enjoying the homecoming game and dance. There's lots of other boys who will want to dance with me."

Katy grinned. "That's right. Let's go."

Katy had chased Shelby and Jewel out of Shelby's room, so she could dress privately. They teased her about her bashfulness, but they had left. Now she reached into her suitcase for the silk bouquet she'd carried in the wedding. She held it in front of her and faced the mirror again. With her free hand, she touched her cheek, then the smoothly combed hair at the nape of her neck, and finally slid her hand down the skirt of her dress. She gave a satisfied nod. *Perfect.* Then she moved to the door and swung it wide.

"Shelby? Jewel? I'm ready."

Footsteps pounded down the hallway, and the pair careened into the room. "It's about time," Jewel complained. "You dress slower than — " Jewel's gaze bounced from Katy's toes to her head. Her mouth fell open.

Shelby folded her arms over her chest and tipped her head to the side, her forehead scrunched. She said, "Are you sure, Katy?"

Katy nodded. "The senior class chose Kathleen Lambright as the sophomore attendant. Well . . ." She looked directly into Jewel's eyes and held her arms outward. "This is the real Kathleen Lambright. I'll be the person God designed me to be no matter what other people think."

"But you're doing what they want," Jewel spluttered. "You're going to make Michael look like a fool."

Katy shook her head, her ribbons flopping wildly against her caped bodice. "No, I'm doing what *I* want. And if they think Michael looks foolish walking in with me, that's *their* problem. I won't change myself because of them. I have to follow my conscience."

A slow smile crept across Jewel's face. She stepped forward and gave a gentle tug on one of the ribbons hanging from Katy's cap. "You've got guts, girlfriend, I'll say that for you." Jewel then laughed. She pinched the sleeve of Katy's dress, her brow puckering. "Is this the dress your new stepmom made?"

"Yes. I packed it to wear to the forensics tournament tomorrow."

Jewel's lips quirked into a saucy smirk. "So are you gonna wear the green dress to the tournament instead?" Katy shook her head wildly, and Jewel laughed again.

Shelby fingered the green dress. "I'm sorry if we made you feel like you couldn't be yourself at homecoming, Katy." She looked worried.

Katy waved her hand. "It wasn't you, Shelby. It was me, trying to figure out what I really wanted. I actually didn't decide for sure until almost the last minute. You're not upset with me, are you?" Even if they were, she wouldn't change.

Jewel said, "Don't sweat it. You gotta be who you gotta be." The girls exchanged a look of understanding.

Katy grinned. "Well, now I'll get out of the way so you two can get ready to go. We're going to have fun, right?"

Katy stood outside the gymnasium doors with the other homecoming royalty, waiting for the announcer to call them in. She heard a few snickers, and Michael Evans stood several feet away from her, but she chose not to let the others bother her. If they couldn't like the real Katy, then they weren't worth worrying about. She set her jaw at a determined angle. *And that goes for Bryce too.*

A hush fell on the other side of the doors, and a voice carried through the loudspeaker: "Ladies and gentlemen, welcome to Salina High North's Homecoming celebration. Please join us in recognizing this year's homecoming royalty." Applause rang and faded. The voice continued, "Beginning with the freshman class attendants, Alana Libel and Logan Allen." The freshmen pair slipped through the doors as the announcer shared, "Alana is the daughter of ..."

Katy's mouth felt dry. She swallowed, but it didn't help. She and Michael would go in next. She glanced at him. He glanced back. She raised her eyebrows and held out her hand. He made a little face, but he stepped close enough for her to slip her hand through the bend of his elbow. Cradling her bouquet with her free hand, she moved forward with Michael as the voice blared, "Our sophomore attendants are Kathleen Lambright and Michael Evans."

Michael's feet moved faster than they'd been advised, so Katy pulled on his arm to slow him down. She listened to the announcer as she held Michael to a slower pace, her heart pounding. "Kathleen is the daughter of Samuel and Rosemary Lambright of Schellberg. She is involved in debate and forensics and recently had an article published in ..." Her activities seemed so much more important when spoken into a microphone and blasted over a loudspeaker. Applause broke out at the completion of her list, and Katy risked a quick glance at the people filling the bleachers to smile in thanks. And her heart nearly stopped beating.

There, on the front row, clapping their palms together in pride and enthusiasm, were Grampa and Gramma, Dad, and Rosemary.

The remainder of the crowning ceremony was a blur. Katy was dimly aware that Tony Adkins was not crowned king. She watched the chosen king and queen receive their crowns from the junior attendants and then share a kiss. But Katy's mind was elsewhere. Dad and Rosemary had come! Instead of leaving for their trip, they'd come to Katy's homecoming! Not until that moment had she realized how much she wanted her family there. And without her even asking them, they'd come.

When the ceremony was over, Katy rushed to her family and bestowed hugs, starting with Gramma and Grampa, then Dad, and finally, hesitantly, Rosemary. Then she turned to Dad again. "What are you doing here? You're supposed to be on your trip."

Dad grinned. "We decided the trip could wait for another day. We wanted to see you." His gaze traveled up and down her length. His expression warmed. "You look beautiful, Katy-girl."

Katy lowered her head in pleasure. Such wonderful

words coming from Dad, who rarely praised. She looked up again. "Thank you. I've never felt more beautiful."

A nervous-sounding *ahem* came from behind Katy. Dad looked past Katy's shoulder, and his brows came down briefly. Then his expression cleared. He tipped toward Katy and whispered, "I think someone would like to speak with you."

Katy turned and found Bryce standing right behind her. Heat filled her ears. She clutched her wedding bouquet to her stomach. "H-hi."

"Hi."

Katy gestured him forward. "Dad, Rosemary, Gramma, Grampa, this is Bryce Porter ... a ... friend."

Each of Katy's family members greeted Bryce by turn, and Bryce shook everyone's hand. Then he turned to her. "I didn't want to interrupt, but could I talk to you for a minute?"

Katy looked back at Dad. Dad seemed to be examining Bryce. Katy wondered what Dad thought of Bryce's navy pleated trousers, tucked-in shirt, and striped tie. Although Bryce wasn't dressed like a Mennonite, his clothes were neat and he looked respectable, unlike a lot of other boys in the school. Even though Bryce had hurt her feelings, Katy didn't want Dad to think badly of him.

Dad put his hand on Rosemary's elbow and gestured toward the gymnasium doors. "We'll step out and get something to drink. Katy, you can find us in the lobby, all right?"

Katy nodded and watched her family leave. Then she turned to Bryce. "What did you want?"

He glanced around, reminding Katy that they stood

in a busy gymnasium crowded with people. He made a face. "Can we at least go out there?" He pointed to the doors where Dad and the others had disappeared. "It'll be quieter."

Katy nodded. But it wasn't quieter, because people were crammed into lines at the concession stand or waiting outside the bathroom.

Bryce sighed. "I know it's kind of chilly, but ...?"

"It's okay. We won't be outside for long."

They headed through the crowd down the hallway. Bryce opened the door for her, and Katy stepped outside. A brisk breeze tossed her ribbons across her cheeks, and she pushed them back. Hugging herself, she looked up at Bryce. Shadows fell over his face, making him look sad and serious. "What did you want?"

"I wanted to finish what I tried to tell you Wednesday after Bible study."

Stupid! The word slammed into Katy's brain. She hugged herself tighter. "Bryce, it's okay. I understand."

"No, you don't." He ran his hand through his hair. "When I said I was stupid, it was because I let some of the guys get to me. Word got around fast that I'd asked you to homecoming, and it didn't take long for the hassling to start. Some of it was pretty ugly. I was embarrassed and mad, and to keep people from bugging me, I just backed off from you." He slipped his hands into his pockets and hunched his shoulders. "But that was stupid. I acted like you'd done something wrong, and you didn't. It was just me. I'm really sorry."

Katy appreciated his apology, but she didn't like that he'd allowed someone else to get in the way of their friendship. If they'd really been friends, no amount of teasing would have changed it.

After a moment, Bryce sighed. "I know you probably won't want to, but I'd still like to sit with you during the game and then go to the dance together. So ... do you ...?" He stood, his head angled to the side, waiting.

Katy drew in a big breath. "I'd like to sit with you during the game. But, Bryce, in my fellowship, dancing is something our leaders discourage. If I go, I'll be disappointing some people who are important to me. And I don't think I'd be pleasing God by ignoring the leaders of my church. So I don't think I should go to the dance."

When she'd rejected Caleb's invitation, he'd gotten mad. So she waited for Bryce to explode with angry words.

"That's okay, Katy." He didn't sound angry at all. Katy nearly wilted with relief. A grin replaced the serious look on his face. "If not the dance, then maybe I could, you know, drive you to Shelby's house after the game?"

He was so cute, especially when he got all pink-faced and bashful. And he did want to be friends after all. Katy decided she could give him another chance. "I'd like that. Very much." Surely Dad wouldn't mind. It was just a car ride after all.

"Great." He grinned. "And maybe we could sit together on the bus tomorrow for the drive to Hill City? We could ... talk?"

Happy flutters made her feel light and airy. She hugged herself. "That sounds good. But can we go inside now? It's cold out here!"

Bryce laughed. "Sure." He opened the door for her, and she skittered inside. They chatted easily on the way back to the gym. Katy spotted her family. "I need to tell my dad and everybody good-bye. I'll meet you in the gym in a minute, okay?"

"Sure, Katy." He trotted off in the direction of the gymnasium.

She watched him until he stepped through the wide doorway, then she dashed to her dad. He held out his arm, and she stepped into his embrace. Katy sighed in contentment. The past weeks hadn't been easy, but she'd learned to be content just being Katy. Snug against Dad's side, she smiled at Rosemary, who smiled back. *Homecoming—I think it might be one of my favorite words.*

Discussion Questions for Katy's Homecoming

1. Were you surprised that Katy was chosen for homecoming attendant? If you were her, would you have wondered why the senior class picked you? Explain.

2. Throughout the book, Katy has to decide for herself whether she should dress and act like everyone at her school, or stay true to her Mennonite upbringing and faith. Have you ever needed to make a decision that really challenged who you are? If so, what did you do?

3. While Katy has accepted Mrs. Graber, she still struggles with all the changes that will come once Mrs. Graber becomes her stepmother. What advice would you give Katy in this situation?

4. Katy, Shelby, and Bryce are all Christians, but they act out their faith in different ways — for instance, Shelby is comfortable wearing a homecoming dress, but Katy agonizes over whether such a dress is appropriate. Do you and your friends (or even family members) have different ways of showing your faith? If so, how do you handle it?

5. Caleb and Annika decide to go to some of the Schellberg youth events together. Do you think this is a good idea? Why or why not? Do you believe Annika when she says she's just having fun with Caleb?

6. While Katy makes the right decision for herself by wearing the dress Mrs. Graber made, would you have done what Katy did? How do you think Michael, her escort, felt? And what do you think would have happened if Katy had worn Cora's green dress to homecoming instead?

A Gift of Grace

A Novel

Amy Clipston

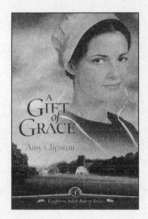

Rebecca Kauffman's tranquil Old Order Amish life is transformed when she suddenly has custody of her two teenage nieces after her "English" sister and brother-in-law are killed in an automobile accident. Instant motherhood, after years of unsuccessful attempts to conceive a child of her own, is both a joy and a heartache. Rebecca struggles to give the teenage girls the guidance they need as well as fulfill her duties to Daniel as an Amish wife.

Rebellious Jessica is resistant to Amish ways and constantly in trouble with the community. Younger sister Lindsay is caught in the middle, and the strain between Rebecca and Daniel mounts as Jessica's rebellion escalates. Instead of the beautiful family life she dreamed of creating for her nieces, Rebecca feels as if her world is being torn apart by two different cultures, leaving her to question her place in the Amish community, her marriage, and her faith in God.

Pick up a copy at your favorite bookstore or online!

Katy's New World

A Novel

Kim Vogel Sawyer

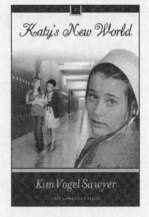

Katy has always enjoyed life in her small Mennonite community, but she longs to learn more than her school can offer. After getting approval from her elders, Katy starts her sophomore year at the public high school in town, where she meets new friends and encounters perspectives very different from her own. But as Katy begins to find her way in the outside world, her relationships at home become strained. Can she find a balance between her two worlds?

Katy's Debate

A Novel

Kim Vogel Sawyer

New Club, New Crush ... New Mom?
Just as Katy is feeling settled in her new
school, everything falls apart at home. Her
father, believing she needs a mother, starts
courting a woman Katy refuses to accept.
Tensions rise as Katy schemes to send the
woman packing. Meanwhile, the pressure builds at school as Katy
joins the debate team, encounters a teammate's scorn, and faces
her growing feelings for a boy her father will never accept. Can
Katy prove she doesn't need a mother's guidance even as she dis-
covers more of what the world offers?

Pick up a copy at your favorite bookstore or online!

Talk It Up!

Want free books?
First looks at the best new fiction?
Awesome exclusive merchandise?

We want to hear from you!

Give us your opinions on titles, covers, and stories.
Join the Z Street Team.

Email us at zstreetteam@zondervan.com
to sign up today!

Also—Friend us on Facebook!

www.facebook.com/goodteenreads

- Video Trailers
- Connect with your favorite authors
- Sneak peeks at new releases
- Giveaways
- Fun discussions
- And much more!